About the Author

Lewis Helfand was born on 27th April 1978 in Philadelphia and grew up in nearby Narberth, Pennsylvania. Although interested in cartoons and animation from a young age, by the time he was twelve, Lewis's focus had turned to writing. After completing high school, he remained in the Philadelphia area with the intention of pursuing a degree in English.

Four years later, with a political science degree and a passion for comic books, Lewis began working for local publishers by proofreading books and newspaper articles. By the age of twenty-four, Lewis had been editing phonebooks for a year and a half, and felt no closer to his lifelong goal of writing comic books. One day, he decided to quit his job.

Lewis then spent the next two months working day and night to write and draw his first comic book, *Wasted Minute*, the story of a world without crime where superheroes are forced to work regular jobs. To cover the cost of self-publishing, he began doing odd jobs in offices and restaurants and started exhibiting his book at local comic-book conventions. With the first issue well received, he was soon collaborating with other artists and released four more issues over the next few years.

At the same time, Lewis continues to work outside the field of comic books as a freelance writer and reporter for a number of national print and online publications. He has covered everything from sports and travel to politics and culture for magazines such as *Renaissance*, *American Health and Fitness*, and *Computer Bits*.

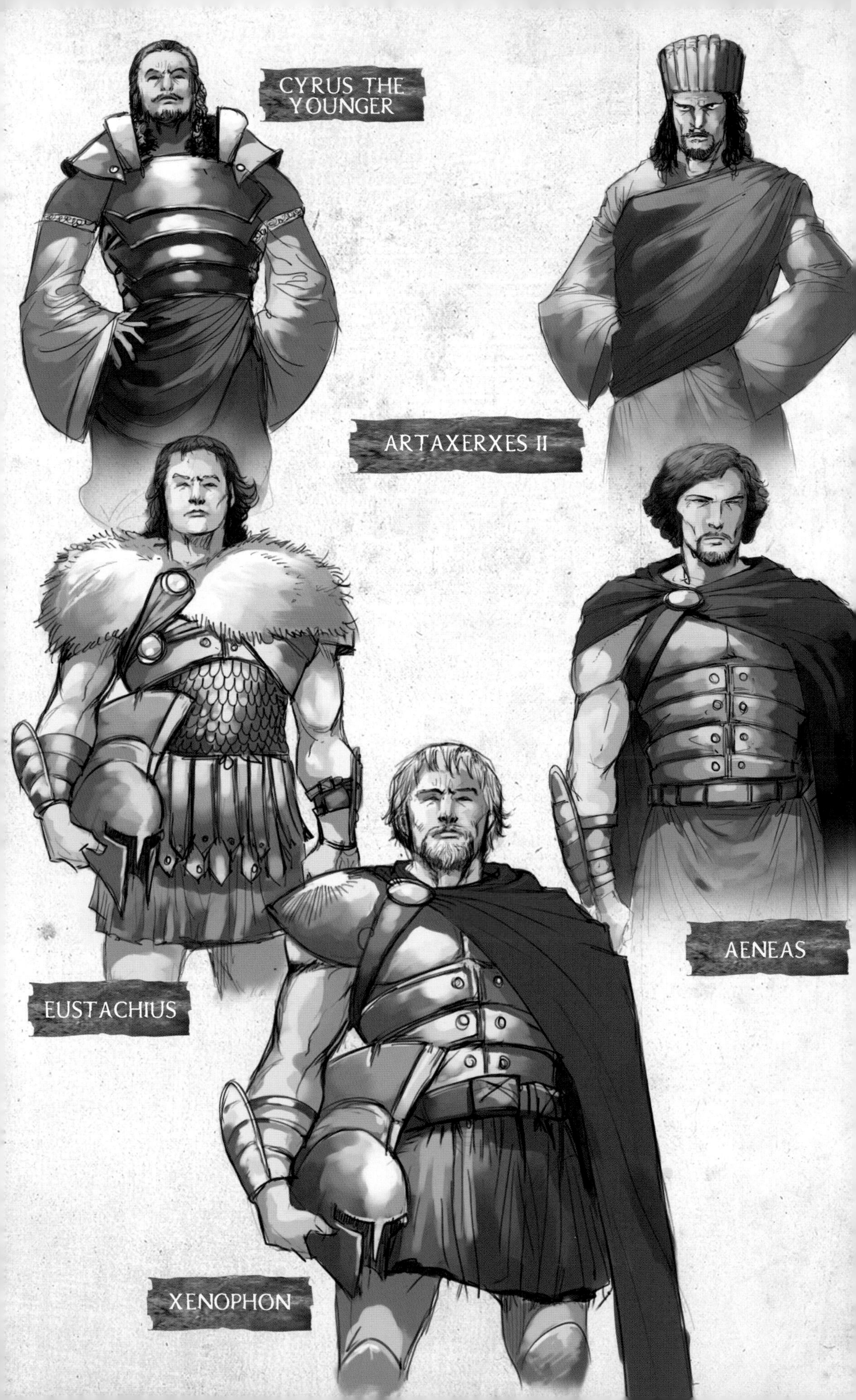
CYRUS THE YOUNGER
ARTAXERXES II
AENEAS
EUSTACHIUS
XENOPHON

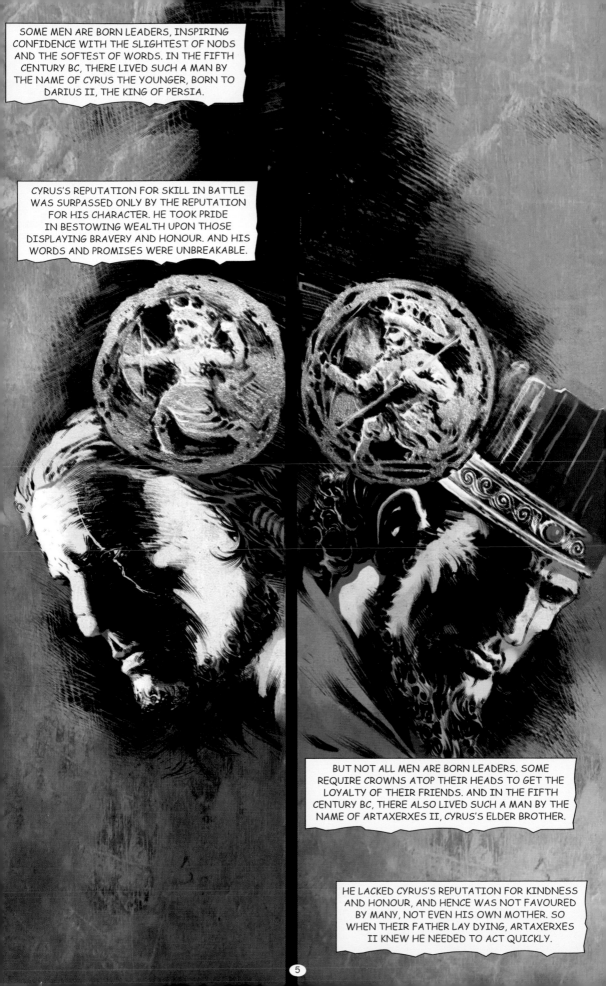

SOME MEN ARE BORN LEADERS, INSPIRING CONFIDENCE WITH THE SLIGHTEST OF NODS AND THE SOFTEST OF WORDS. IN THE FIFTH CENTURY BC, THERE LIVED SUCH A MAN BY THE NAME OF CYRUS THE YOUNGER, BORN TO DARIUS II, THE KING OF PERSIA.

CYRUS'S REPUTATION FOR SKILL IN BATTLE WAS SURPASSED ONLY BY THE REPUTATION FOR HIS CHARACTER. HE TOOK PRIDE IN BESTOWING WEALTH UPON THOSE DISPLAYING BRAVERY AND HONOUR. AND HIS WORDS AND PROMISES WERE UNBREAKABLE.

BUT NOT ALL MEN ARE BORN LEADERS. SOME REQUIRE CROWNS ATOP THEIR HEADS TO GET THE LOYALTY OF THEIR FRIENDS. AND IN THE FIFTH CENTURY BC, THERE ALSO LIVED SUCH A MAN BY THE NAME OF ARTAXERXES II, CYRUS'S ELDER BROTHER.

HE LACKED CYRUS'S REPUTATION FOR KINDNESS AND HONOUR, AND HENCE WAS NOT FAVOURED BY MANY, NOT EVEN HIS OWN MOTHER. SO WHEN THEIR FATHER LAY DYING, ARTAXERXES II KNEW HE NEEDED TO ACT QUICKLY.

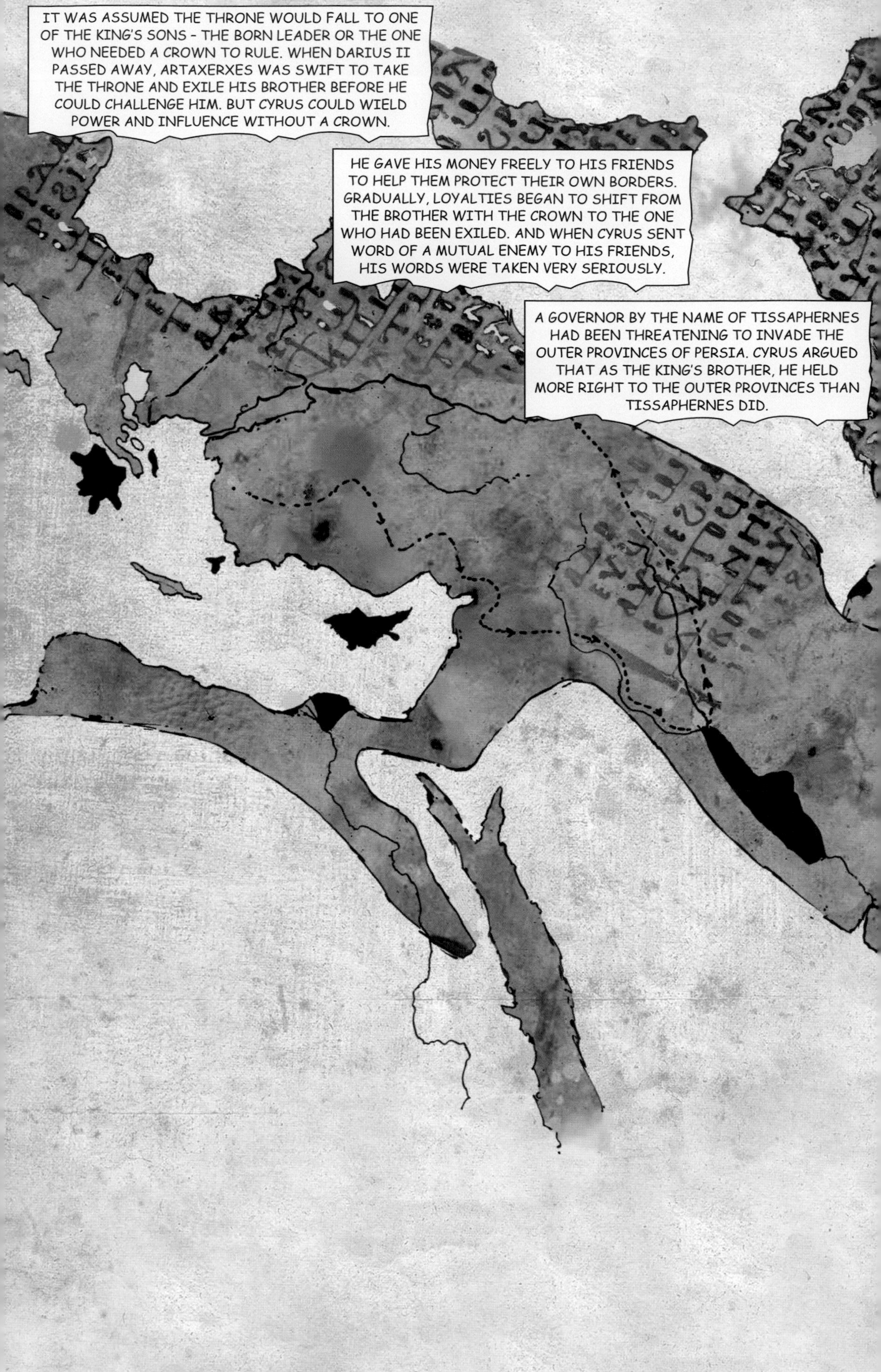
IT WAS ASSUMED THE THRONE WOULD FALL TO ONE OF THE KING'S SONS - THE BORN LEADER OR THE ONE WHO NEEDED A CROWN TO RULE. WHEN DARIUS II PASSED AWAY, ARTAXERXES WAS SWIFT TO TAKE THE THRONE AND EXILE HIS BROTHER BEFORE HE COULD CHALLENGE HIM. BUT CYRUS COULD WIELD POWER AND INFLUENCE WITHOUT A CROWN.
HE GAVE HIS MONEY FREELY TO HIS FRIENDS TO HELP THEM PROTECT THEIR OWN BORDERS. GRADUALLY, LOYALTIES BEGAN TO SHIFT FROM THE BROTHER WITH THE CROWN TO THE ONE WHO HAD BEEN EXILED. AND WHEN CYRUS SENT WORD OF A MUTUAL ENEMY TO HIS FRIENDS, HIS WORDS WERE TAKEN VERY SERIOUSLY.
A GOVERNOR BY THE NAME OF TISSAPHERNES HAD BEEN THREATENING TO INVADE THE OUTER PROVINCES OF PERSIA. CYRUS ARGUED THAT AS THE KING'S BROTHER, HE HELD MORE RIGHT TO THE OUTER PROVINCES THAN TISSAPHERNES DID.

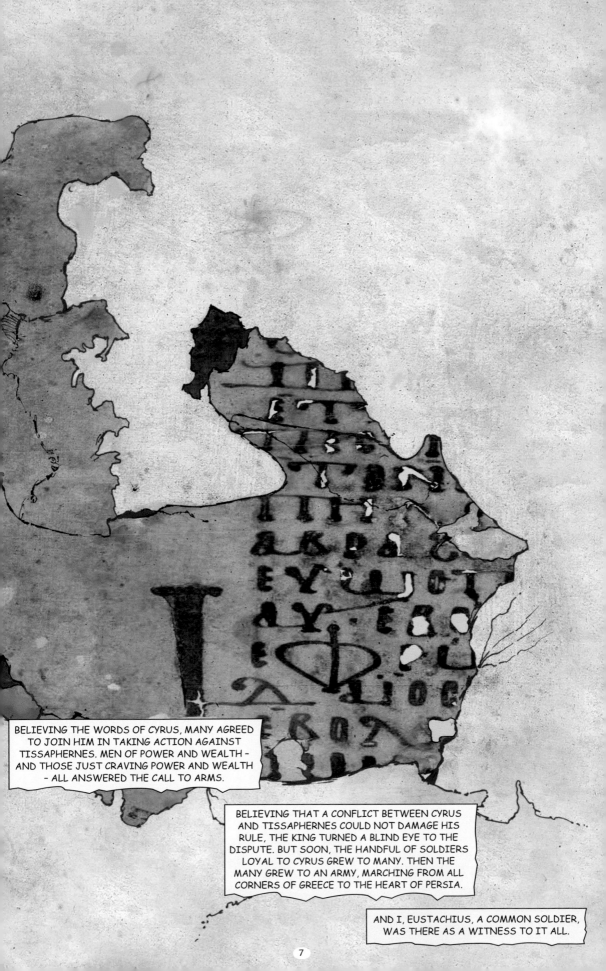

BELIEVING THE WORDS OF CYRUS, MANY AGREED TO JOIN HIM IN TAKING ACTION AGAINST TISSAPHERNES. MEN OF POWER AND WEALTH – AND THOSE JUST CRAVING POWER AND WEALTH – ALL ANSWERED THE CALL TO ARMS.

BELIEVING THAT A CONFLICT BETWEEN CYRUS AND TISSAPHERNES COULD NOT DAMAGE HIS RULE, THE KING TURNED A BLIND EYE TO THE DISPUTE. BUT SOON, THE HANDFUL OF SOLDIERS LOYAL TO CYRUS GREW TO MANY. THEN THE MANY GREW TO AN ARMY, MARCHING FROM ALL CORNERS OF GREECE TO THE HEART OF PERSIA.

AND I, EUSTACHIUS, A COMMON SOLDIER, WAS THERE AS A WITNESS TO IT ALL.

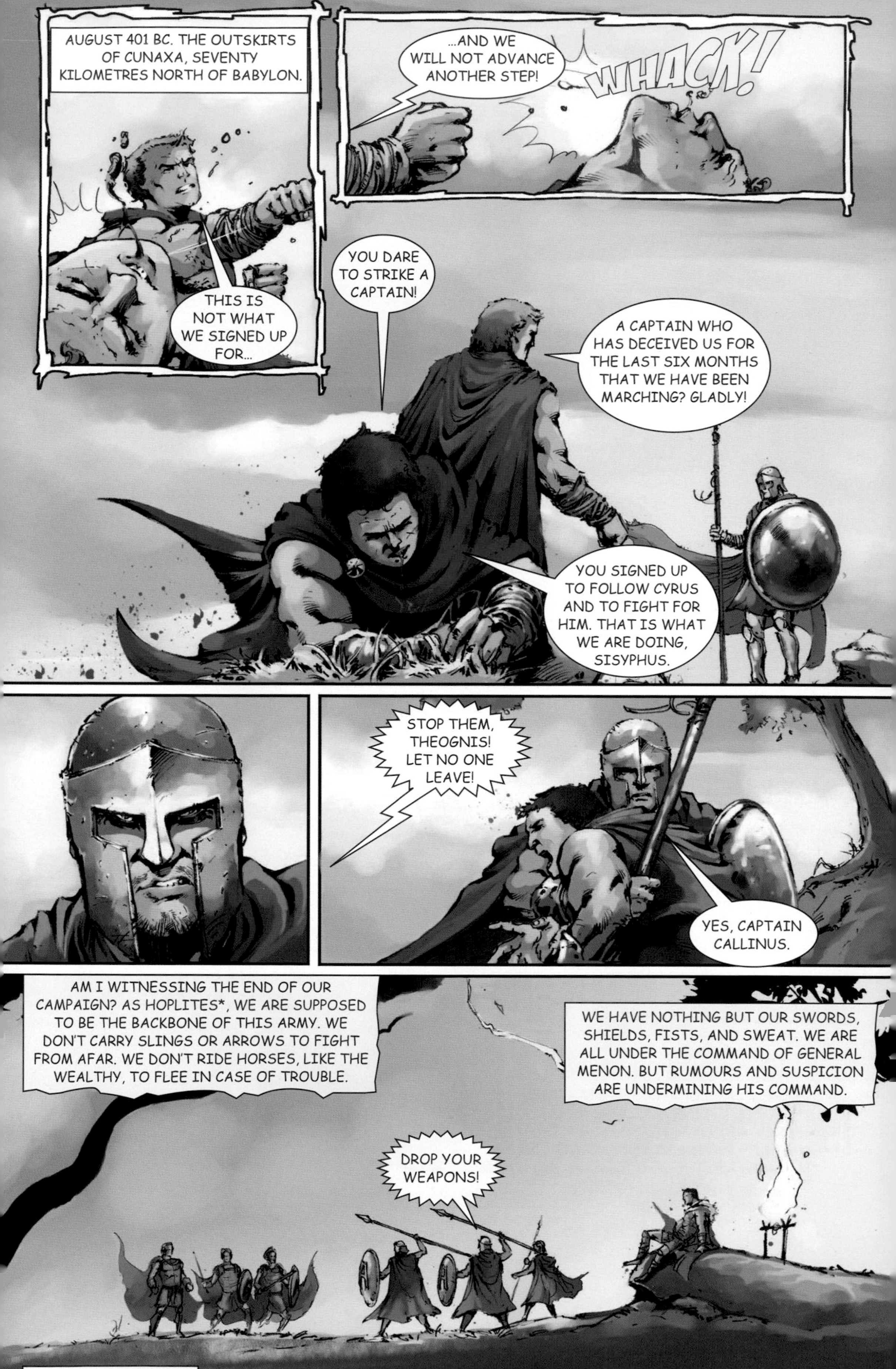
AUGUST 401 BC. THE OUTSKIRTS OF CUNAXA, SEVENTY KILOMETRES NORTH OF BABYLON.
THIS IS NOT WHAT WE SIGNED UP FOR...
...AND WE WILL NOT ADVANCE ANOTHER STEP!
WHACK!
YOU DARE TO STRIKE A CAPTAIN!
A CAPTAIN WHO HAS DECEIVED US FOR THE LAST SIX MONTHS THAT WE HAVE BEEN MARCHING? GLADLY!
YOU SIGNED UP TO FOLLOW CYRUS AND TO FIGHT FOR HIM. THAT IS WHAT WE ARE DOING, SISYPHUS.
STOP THEM, THEOGNIS! LET NO ONE LEAVE!
YES, CAPTAIN CALLINUS.
AM I WITNESSING THE END OF OUR CAMPAIGN? AS HOPLITES*, WE ARE SUPPOSED TO BE THE BACKBONE OF THIS ARMY. WE DON'T CARRY SLINGS OR ARROWS TO FIGHT FROM AFAR. WE DON'T RIDE HORSES, LIKE THE WEALTHY, TO FLEE IN CASE OF TROUBLE.
WE HAVE NOTHING BUT OUR SWORDS, SHIELDS, FISTS, AND SWEAT. WE ARE ALL UNDER THE COMMAND OF GENERAL MENON. BUT RUMOURS AND SUSPICION ARE UNDERMINING HIS COMMAND.
DROP YOUR WEAPONS!

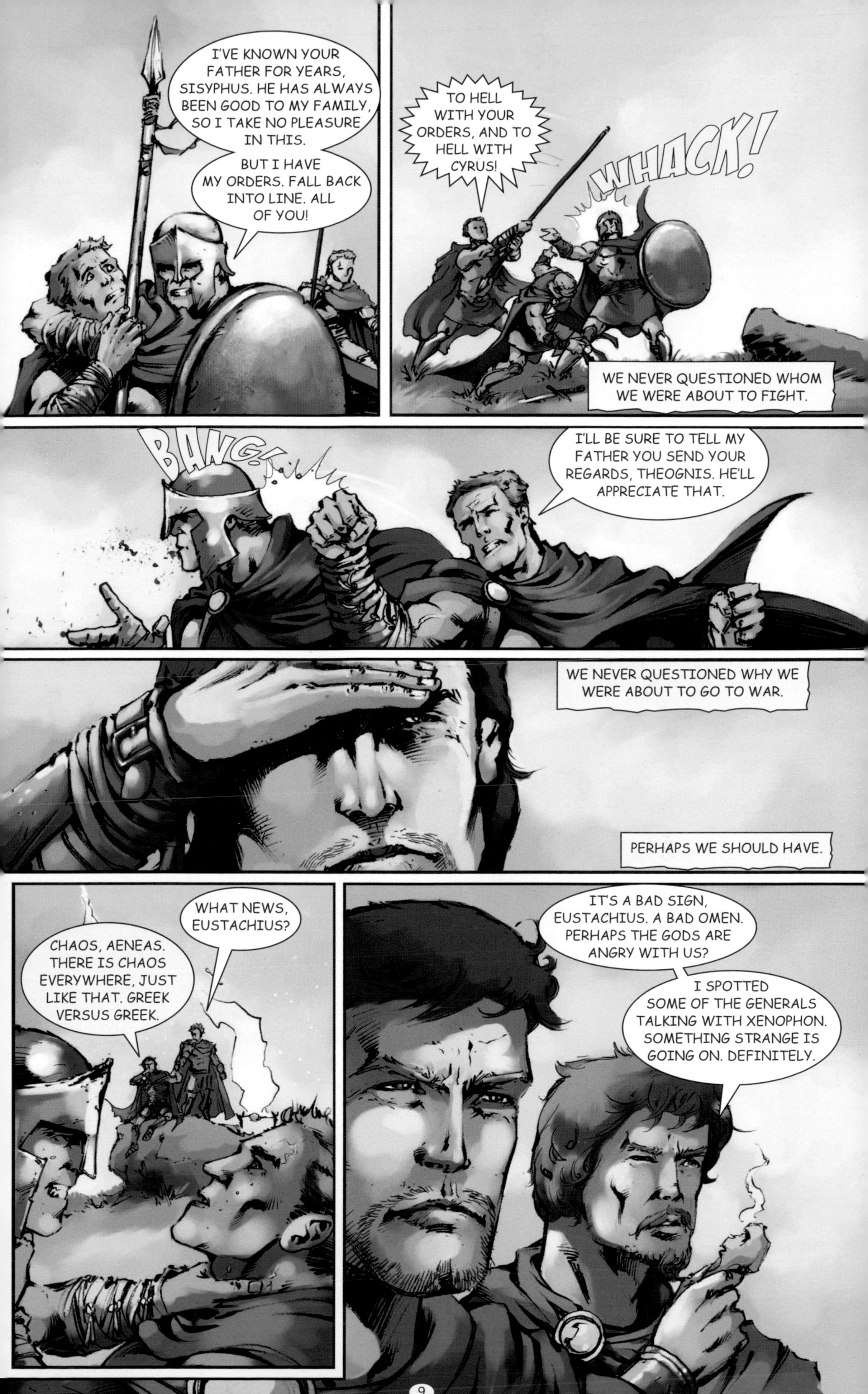
I'VE KNOWN YOUR FATHER FOR YEARS, SISYPHUS. HE HAS ALWAYS BEEN GOOD TO MY FAMILY, SO I TAKE NO PLEASURE IN THIS.
BUT I HAVE MY ORDERS. FALL BACK INTO LINE. ALL OF YOU!
TO HELL WITH YOUR ORDERS, AND TO HELL WITH CYRUS!
WHACK!
WE NEVER QUESTIONED WHOM WE WERE ABOUT TO FIGHT.
BANG!
I'LL BE SURE TO TELL MY FATHER YOU SEND YOUR REGARDS, THEOGNIS. HE'LL APPRECIATE THAT.
WE NEVER QUESTIONED WHY WE WERE ABOUT TO GO TO WAR.
PERHAPS WE SHOULD HAVE.
WHAT NEWS, EUSTACHIUS?
CHAOS, AENEAS. THERE IS CHAOS EVERYWHERE, JUST LIKE THAT. GREEK VERSUS GREEK.
IT'S A BAD SIGN, EUSTACHIUS. A BAD OMEN. PERHAPS THE GODS ARE ANGRY WITH US?
I SPOTTED SOME OF THE GENERALS TALKING WITH XENOPHON. SOMETHING STRANGE IS GOING ON. DEFINITELY.

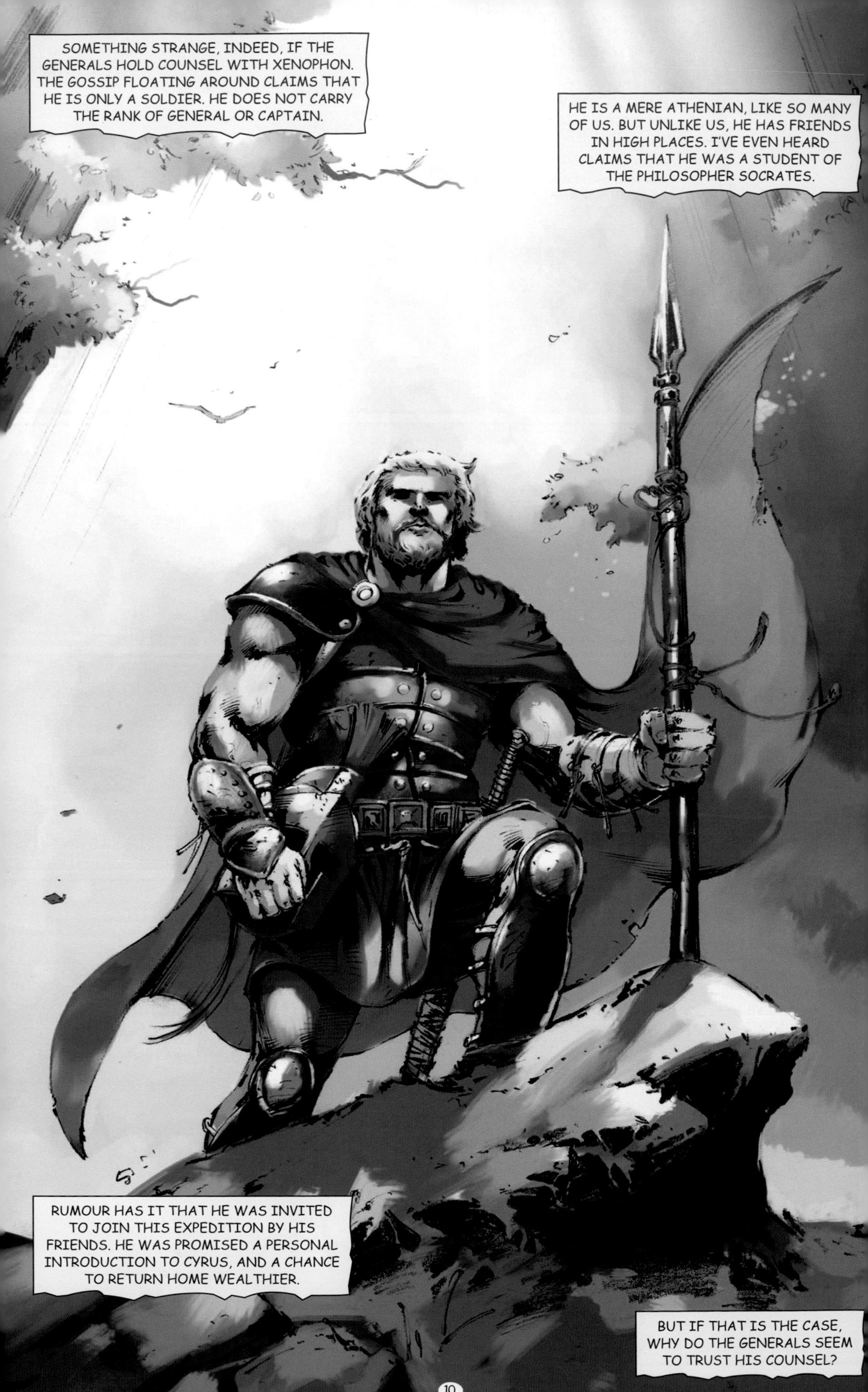
SOMETHING STRANGE, INDEED, IF THE GENERALS HOLD COUNSEL WITH XENOPHON. THE GOSSIP FLOATING AROUND CLAIMS THAT HE IS ONLY A SOLDIER. HE DOES NOT CARRY THE RANK OF GENERAL OR CAPTAIN.
HE IS A MERE ATHENIAN, LIKE SO MANY OF US. BUT UNLIKE US, HE HAS FRIENDS IN HIGH PLACES. I'VE EVEN HEARD CLAIMS THAT HE WAS A STUDENT OF THE PHILOSOPHER SOCRATES.
RUMOUR HAS IT THAT HE WAS INVITED TO JOIN THIS EXPEDITION BY HIS FRIENDS. HE WAS PROMISED A PERSONAL INTRODUCTION TO CYRUS, AND A CHANCE TO RETURN HOME WEALTHIER.
BUT IF THAT IS THE CASE, WHY DO THE GENERALS SEEM TO TRUST HIS COUNSEL?

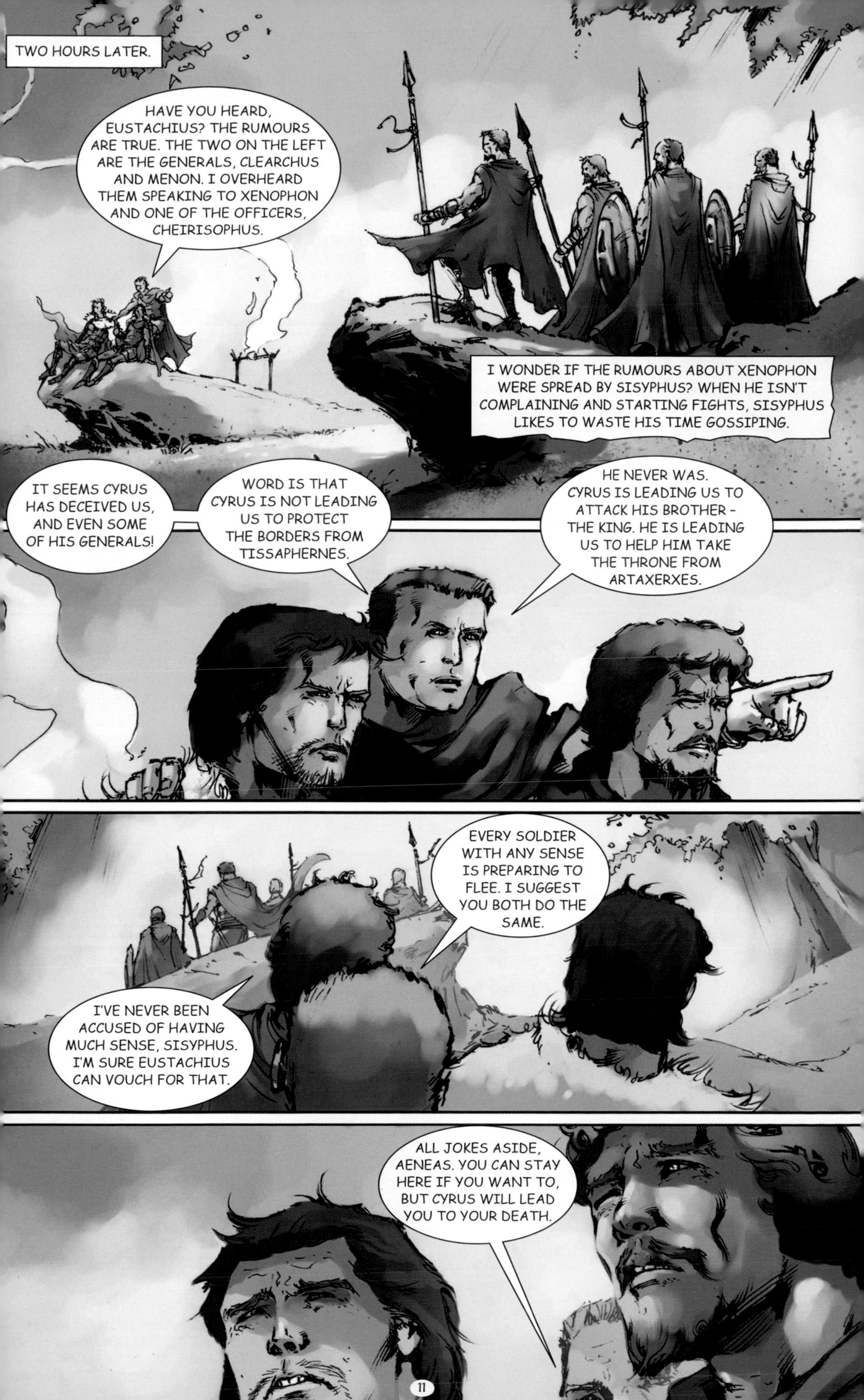
TWO HOURS LATER.
HAVE YOU HEARD, EUSTACHIUS? THE RUMOURS ARE TRUE. THE TWO ON THE LEFT ARE THE GENERALS, CLEARCHUS AND MENON. I OVERHEARD THEM SPEAKING TO XENOPHON AND ONE OF THE OFFICERS, CHEIRISOPHUS.
I WONDER IF THE RUMOURS ABOUT XENOPHON WERE SPREAD BY SISYPHUS? WHEN HE ISN'T COMPLAINING AND STARTING FIGHTS, SISYPHUS LIKES TO WASTE HIS TIME GOSSIPING.
IT SEEMS CYRUS HAS DECEIVED US, AND EVEN SOME OF HIS GENERALS!
WORD IS THAT CYRUS IS NOT LEADING US TO PROTECT THE BORDERS FROM TISSAPHERNES.
HE NEVER WAS. CYRUS IS LEADING US TO ATTACK HIS BROTHER - THE KING. HE IS LEADING US TO HELP HIM TAKE THE THRONE FROM ARTAXERXES.
EVERY SOLDIER WITH ANY SENSE IS PREPARING TO FLEE. I SUGGEST YOU BOTH DO THE SAME.
I'VE NEVER BEEN ACCUSED OF HAVING MUCH SENSE, SISYPHUS. I'M SURE EUSTACHIUS CAN VOUCH FOR THAT.
ALL JOKES ASIDE, AENEAS. YOU CAN STAY HERE IF YOU WANT TO, BUT CYRUS WILL LEAD YOU TO YOUR DEATH.

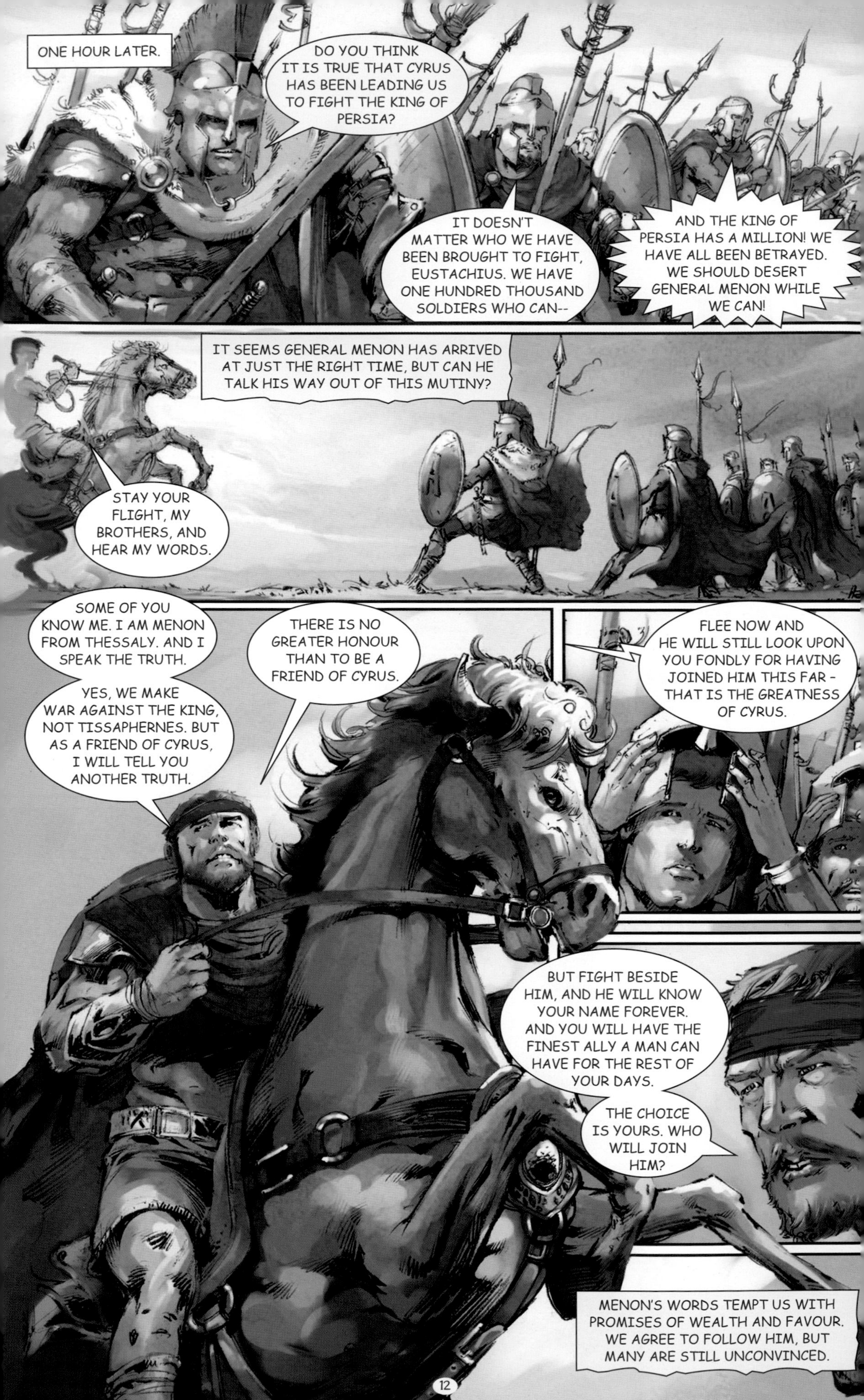

ONE HOUR LATER.
DO YOU THINK IT IS TRUE THAT CYRUS HAS BEEN LEADING US TO FIGHT THE KING OF PERSIA?
IT DOESN'T MATTER WHO WE HAVE BEEN BROUGHT TO FIGHT, EUSTACHIUS. WE HAVE ONE HUNDRED THOUSAND SOLDIERS WHO CAN--
AND THE KING OF PERSIA HAS A MILLION! WE HAVE ALL BEEN BETRAYED. WE SHOULD DESERT GENERAL MENON WHILE WE CAN!
IT SEEMS GENERAL MENON HAS ARRIVED AT JUST THE RIGHT TIME, BUT CAN HE TALK HIS WAY OUT OF THIS MUTINY?
STAY YOUR FLIGHT, MY BROTHERS, AND HEAR MY WORDS.
SOME OF YOU KNOW ME. I AM MENON FROM THESSALY. AND I SPEAK THE TRUTH.
YES, WE MAKE WAR AGAINST THE KING, NOT TISSAPHERNES. BUT AS A FRIEND OF CYRUS, I WILL TELL YOU ANOTHER TRUTH.
THERE IS NO GREATER HONOUR THAN TO BE A FRIEND OF CYRUS.
FLEE NOW AND HE WILL STILL LOOK UPON YOU FONDLY FOR HAVING JOINED HIM THIS FAR – THAT IS THE GREATNESS OF CYRUS.
BUT FIGHT BESIDE HIM, AND HE WILL KNOW YOUR NAME FOREVER. AND YOU WILL HAVE THE FINEST ALLY A MAN CAN HAVE FOR THE REST OF YOUR DAYS.
THE CHOICE IS YOURS. WHO WILL JOIN HIM?
MENON'S WORDS TEMPT US WITH PROMISES OF WEALTH AND FAVOUR. WE AGREE TO FOLLOW HIM, BUT MANY ARE STILL UNCONVINCED.

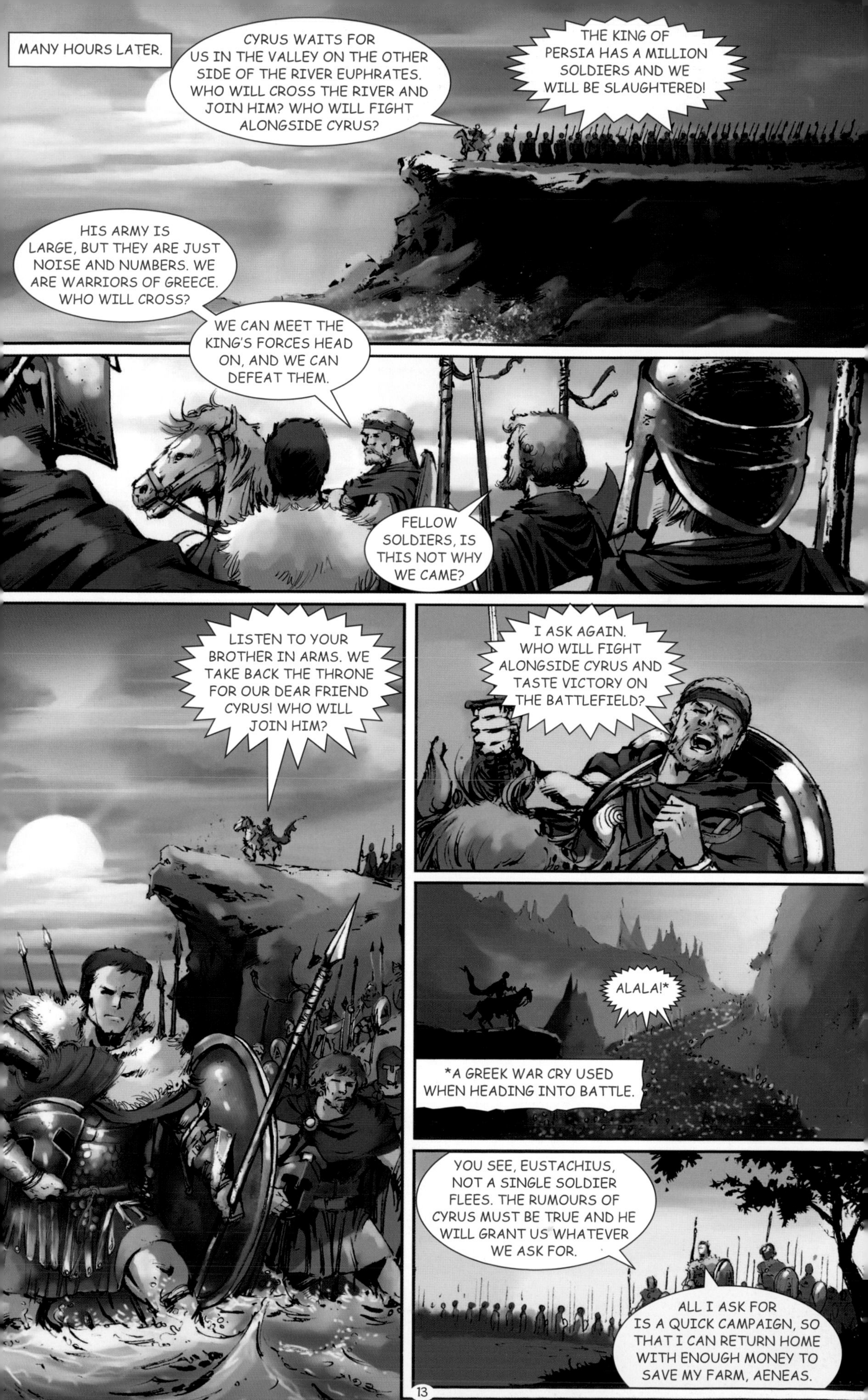

MANY HOURS LATER.
CYRUS WAITS FOR US IN THE VALLEY ON THE OTHER SIDE OF THE RIVER EUPHRATES. WHO WILL CROSS THE RIVER AND JOIN HIM? WHO WILL FIGHT ALONGSIDE CYRUS?
THE KING OF PERSIA HAS A MILLION SOLDIERS AND WE WILL BE SLAUGHTERED!
HIS ARMY IS LARGE, BUT THEY ARE JUST NOISE AND NUMBERS. WE ARE WARRIORS OF GREECE. WHO WILL CROSS?
WE CAN MEET THE KING'S FORCES HEAD ON, AND WE CAN DEFEAT THEM.
FELLOW SOLDIERS, IS THIS NOT WHY WE CAME?
LISTEN TO YOUR BROTHER IN ARMS. WE TAKE BACK THE THRONE FOR OUR DEAR FRIEND CYRUS! WHO WILL JOIN HIM?
I ASK AGAIN. WHO WILL FIGHT ALONGSIDE CYRUS AND TASTE VICTORY ON THE BATTLEFIELD?
ALALA!*
*A GREEK WAR CRY USED WHEN HEADING INTO BATTLE.
YOU SEE, EUSTACHIUS, NOT A SINGLE SOLDIER FLEES. THE RUMOURS OF CYRUS MUST BE TRUE AND HE WILL GRANT US WHATEVER WE ASK FOR.
ALL I ASK FOR IS A QUICK CAMPAIGN, SO THAT I CAN RETURN HOME WITH ENOUGH MONEY TO SAVE MY FARM, AENEAS.

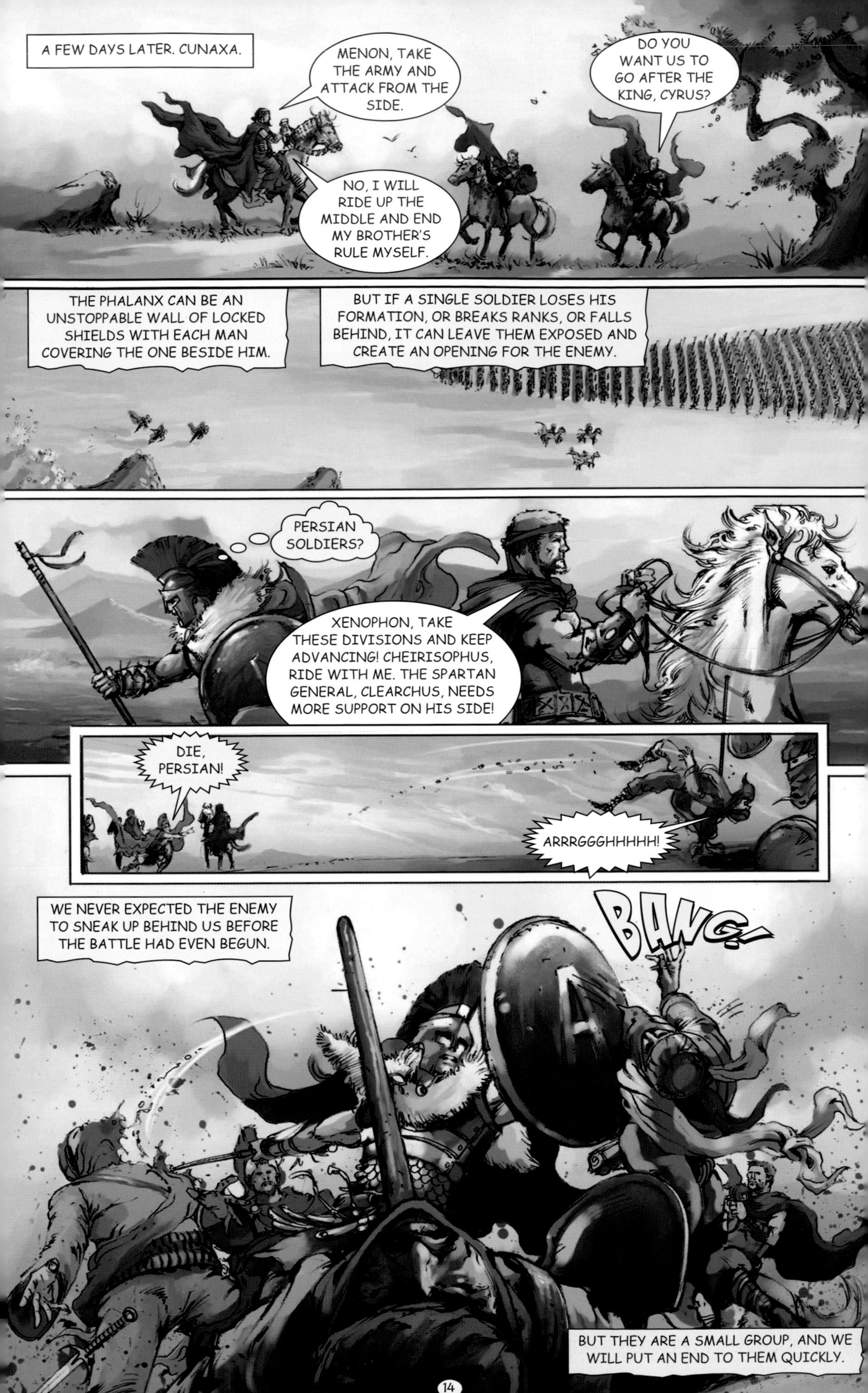

A FEW DAYS LATER. CUNAXA.
MENON, TAKE THE ARMY AND ATTACK FROM THE SIDE.
DO YOU WANT US TO GO AFTER THE KING, CYRUS?
NO, I WILL RIDE UP THE MIDDLE AND END MY BROTHER'S RULE MYSELF.
THE PHALANX CAN BE AN UNSTOPPABLE WALL OF LOCKED SHIELDS WITH EACH MAN COVERING THE ONE BESIDE HIM.
BUT IF A SINGLE SOLDIER LOSES HIS FORMATION, OR BREAKS RANKS, OR FALLS BEHIND, IT CAN LEAVE THEM EXPOSED AND CREATE AN OPENING FOR THE ENEMY.
PERSIAN SOLDIERS?
XENOPHON, TAKE THESE DIVISIONS AND KEEP ADVANCING! CHEIRISOPHUS, RIDE WITH ME. THE SPARTAN GENERAL, CLEARCHUS, NEEDS MORE SUPPORT ON HIS SIDE!
DIE, PERSIAN!
ARRRGGGHHHHH!
WE NEVER EXPECTED THE ENEMY TO SNEAK UP BEHIND US BEFORE THE BATTLE HAD EVEN BEGUN.
BANG!
BUT THEY ARE A SMALL GROUP, AND WE WILL PUT AN END TO THEM QUICKLY.

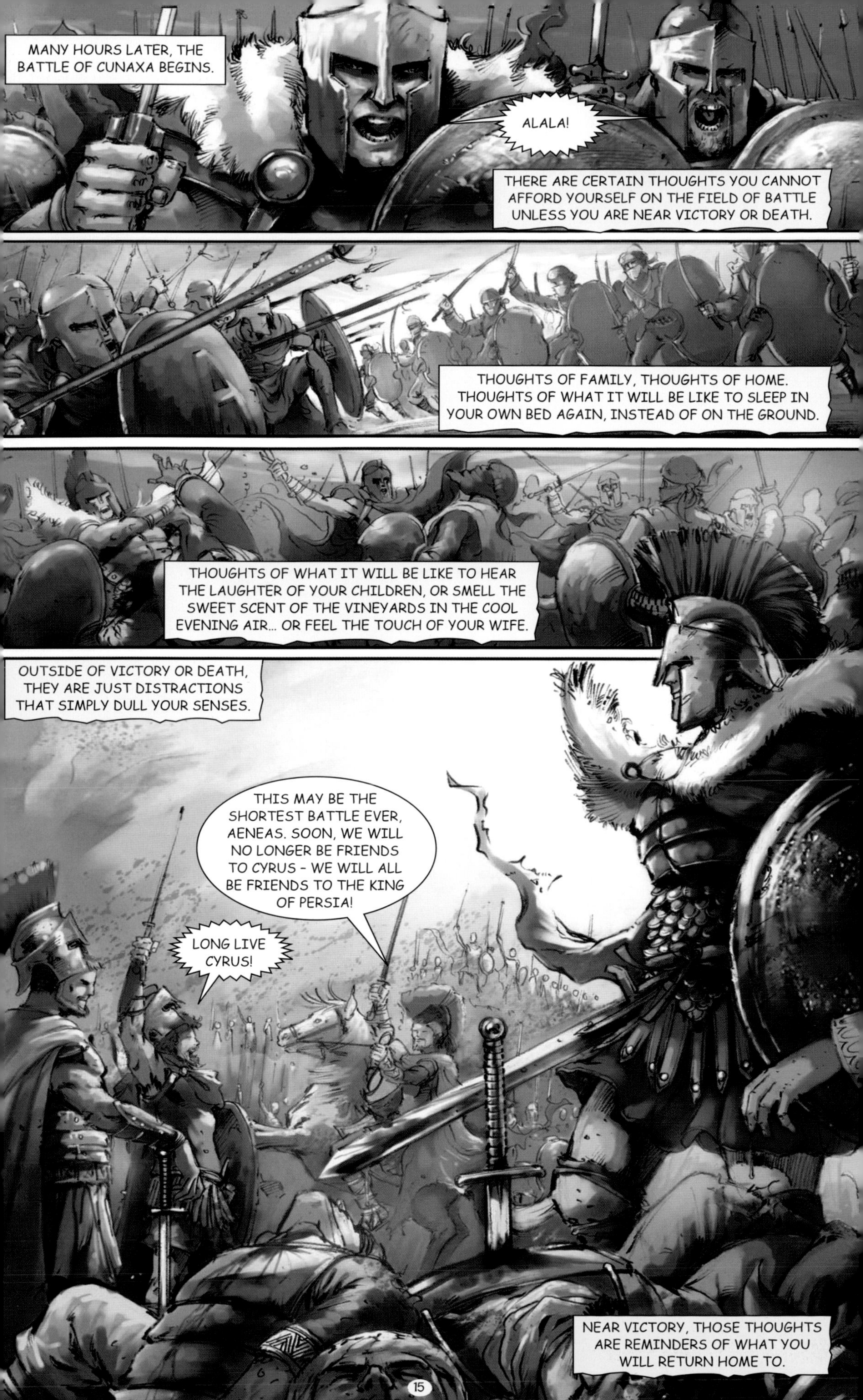
MANY HOURS LATER, THE BATTLE OF CUNAXA BEGINS.
ALALA!
THERE ARE CERTAIN THOUGHTS YOU CANNOT AFFORD YOURSELF ON THE FIELD OF BATTLE UNLESS YOU ARE NEAR VICTORY OR DEATH.
THOUGHTS OF FAMILY, THOUGHTS OF HOME. THOUGHTS OF WHAT IT WILL BE LIKE TO SLEEP IN YOUR OWN BED AGAIN, INSTEAD OF ON THE GROUND.
THOUGHTS OF WHAT IT WILL BE LIKE TO HEAR THE LAUGHTER OF YOUR CHILDREN, OR SMELL THE SWEET SCENT OF THE VINEYARDS IN THE COOL EVENING AIR... OR FEEL THE TOUCH OF YOUR WIFE.
OUTSIDE OF VICTORY OR DEATH, THEY ARE JUST DISTRACTIONS THAT SIMPLY DULL YOUR SENSES.
THIS MAY BE THE SHORTEST BATTLE EVER, AENEAS. SOON, WE WILL NO LONGER BE FRIENDS TO CYRUS - WE WILL ALL BE FRIENDS TO THE KING OF PERSIA!
LONG LIVE CYRUS!
NEAR VICTORY, THOSE THOUGHTS ARE REMINDERS OF WHAT YOU WILL RETURN HOME TO.

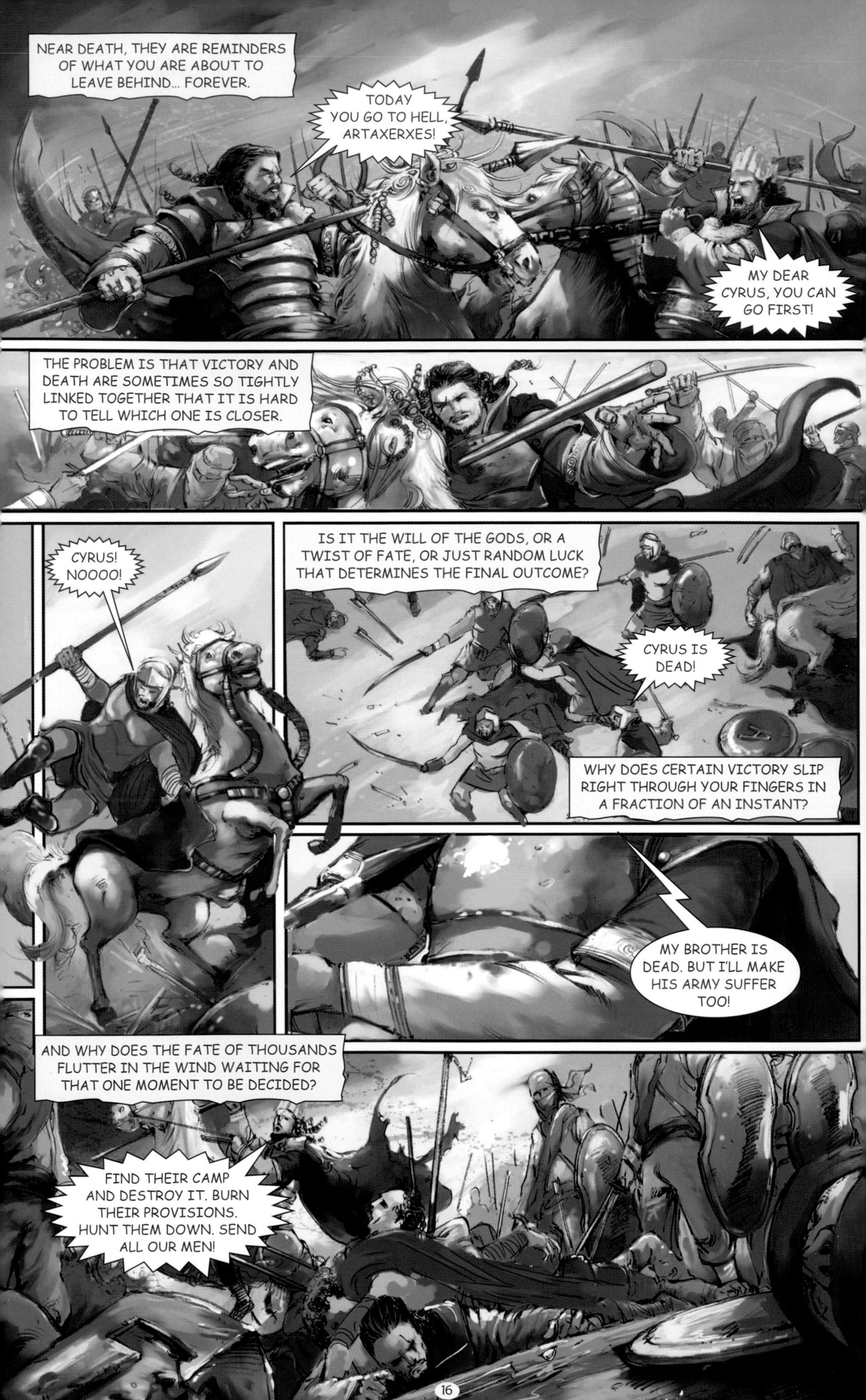
NEAR DEATH, THEY ARE REMINDERS OF WHAT YOU ARE ABOUT TO LEAVE BEHIND... FOREVER.
TODAY YOU GO TO HELL, ARTAXERXES!
MY DEAR CYRUS, YOU CAN GO FIRST!
THE PROBLEM IS THAT VICTORY AND DEATH ARE SOMETIMES SO TIGHTLY LINKED TOGETHER THAT IT IS HARD TO TELL WHICH ONE IS CLOSER.
CYRUS! NOOOO!
IS IT THE WILL OF THE GODS, OR A TWIST OF FATE, OR JUST RANDOM LUCK THAT DETERMINES THE FINAL OUTCOME?
CYRUS IS DEAD!
WHY DOES CERTAIN VICTORY SLIP RIGHT THROUGH YOUR FINGERS IN A FRACTION OF AN INSTANT?
MY BROTHER IS DEAD. BUT I'LL MAKE HIS ARMY SUFFER TOO!
AND WHY DOES THE FATE OF THOUSANDS FLUTTER IN THE WIND WAITING FOR THAT ONE MOMENT TO BE DECIDED?
FIND THEIR CAMP AND DESTROY IT. BURN THEIR PROVISIONS. HUNT THEM DOWN. SEND ALL OUR MEN!

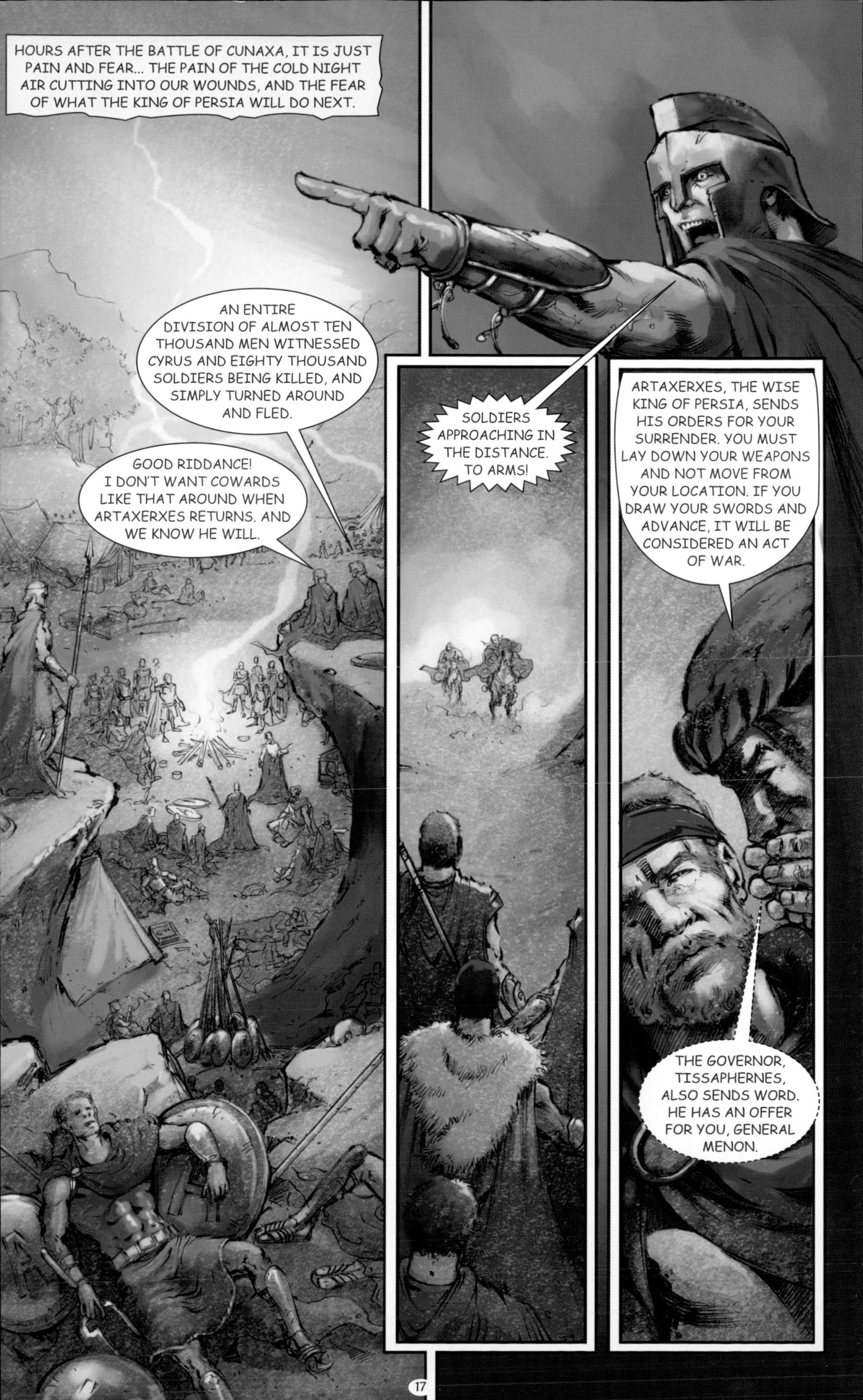
HOURS AFTER THE BATTLE OF CUNAXA, IT IS JUST PAIN AND FEAR... THE PAIN OF THE COLD NIGHT AIR CUTTING INTO OUR WOUNDS, AND THE FEAR OF WHAT THE KING OF PERSIA WILL DO NEXT.
AN ENTIRE DIVISION OF ALMOST TEN THOUSAND MEN WITNESSED CYRUS AND EIGHTY THOUSAND SOLDIERS BEING KILLED, AND SIMPLY TURNED AROUND AND FLED.
GOOD RIDDANCE! I DON'T WANT COWARDS LIKE THAT AROUND WHEN ARTAXERXES RETURNS. AND WE KNOW HE WILL.
SOLDIERS APPROACHING IN THE DISTANCE. TO ARMS!
ARTAXERXES, THE WISE KING OF PERSIA, SENDS HIS ORDERS FOR YOUR SURRENDER. YOU MUST LAY DOWN YOUR WEAPONS AND NOT MOVE FROM YOUR LOCATION. IF YOU DRAW YOUR SWORDS AND ADVANCE, IT WILL BE CONSIDERED AN ACT OF WAR.
THE GOVERNOR, TISSAPHERNES, ALSO SENDS WORD. HE HAS AN OFFER FOR YOU, GENERAL MENON.

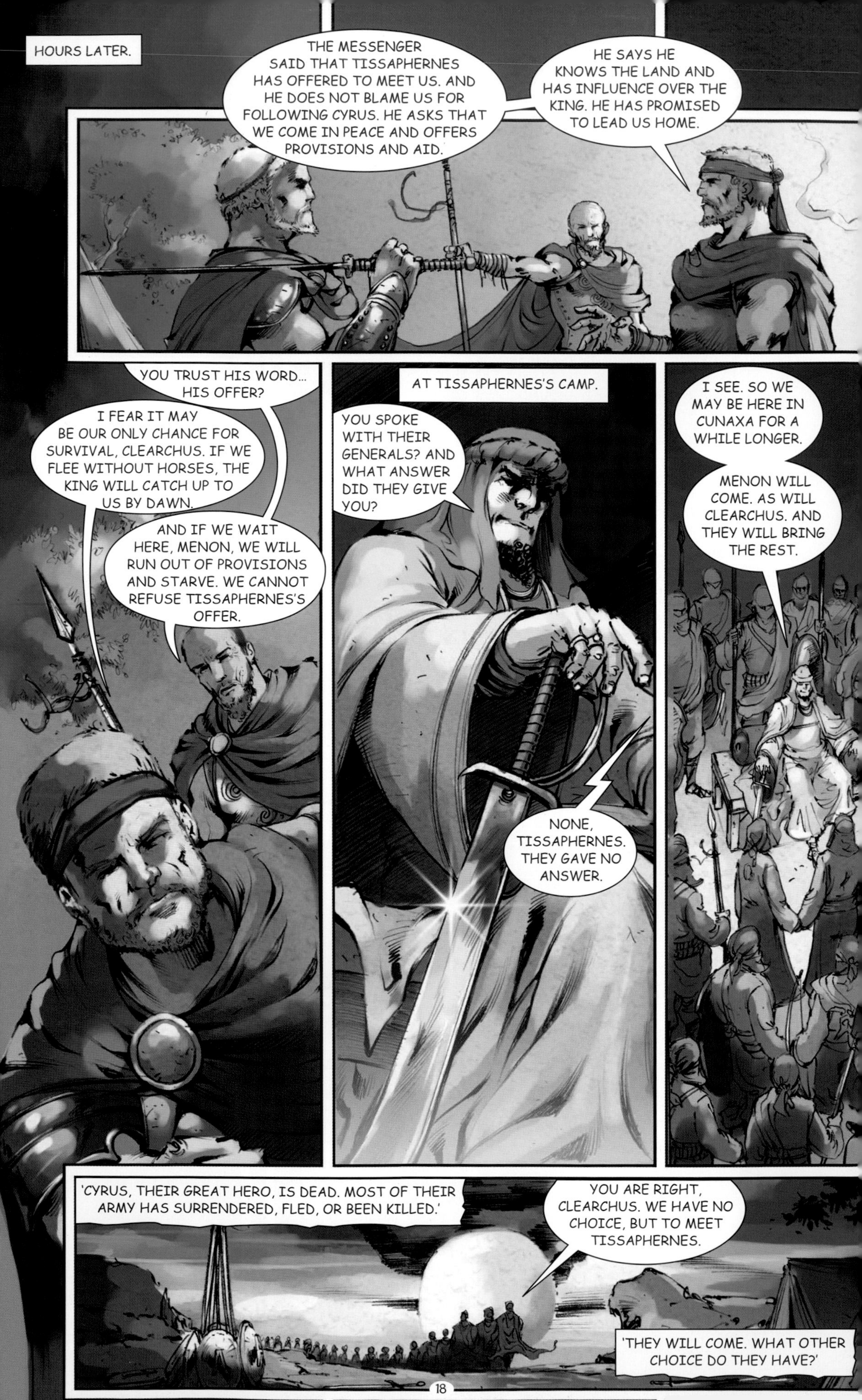
HOURS LATER.
THE MESSENGER SAID THAT TISSAPHERNES HAS OFFERED TO MEET US. AND HE DOES NOT BLAME US FOR FOLLOWING CYRUS. HE ASKS THAT WE COME IN PEACE AND OFFERS PROVISIONS AND AID.
HE SAYS HE KNOWS THE LAND AND HAS INFLUENCE OVER THE KING. HE HAS PROMISED TO LEAD US HOME.
YOU TRUST HIS WORD... HIS OFFER?
I FEAR IT MAY BE OUR ONLY CHANCE FOR SURVIVAL, CLEARCHUS. IF WE FLEE WITHOUT HORSES, THE KING WILL CATCH UP TO US BY DAWN.
AND IF WE WAIT HERE, MENON, WE WILL RUN OUT OF PROVISIONS AND STARVE. WE CANNOT REFUSE TISSAPHERNES'S OFFER.
AT TISSAPHERNES'S CAMP.
YOU SPOKE WITH THEIR GENERALS? AND WHAT ANSWER DID THEY GIVE YOU?
NONE, TISSAPHERNES. THEY GAVE NO ANSWER.
I SEE. SO WE MAY BE HERE IN CUNAXA FOR A WHILE LONGER.
MENON WILL COME. AS WILL CLEARCHUS. AND THEY WILL BRING THE REST.
'CYRUS, THEIR GREAT HERO, IS DEAD. MOST OF THEIR ARMY HAS SURRENDERED, FLED, OR BEEN KILLED.'
YOU ARE RIGHT, CLEARCHUS. WE HAVE NO CHOICE, BUT TO MEET TISSAPHERNES.
'THEY WILL COME. WHAT OTHER CHOICE DO THEY HAVE?'

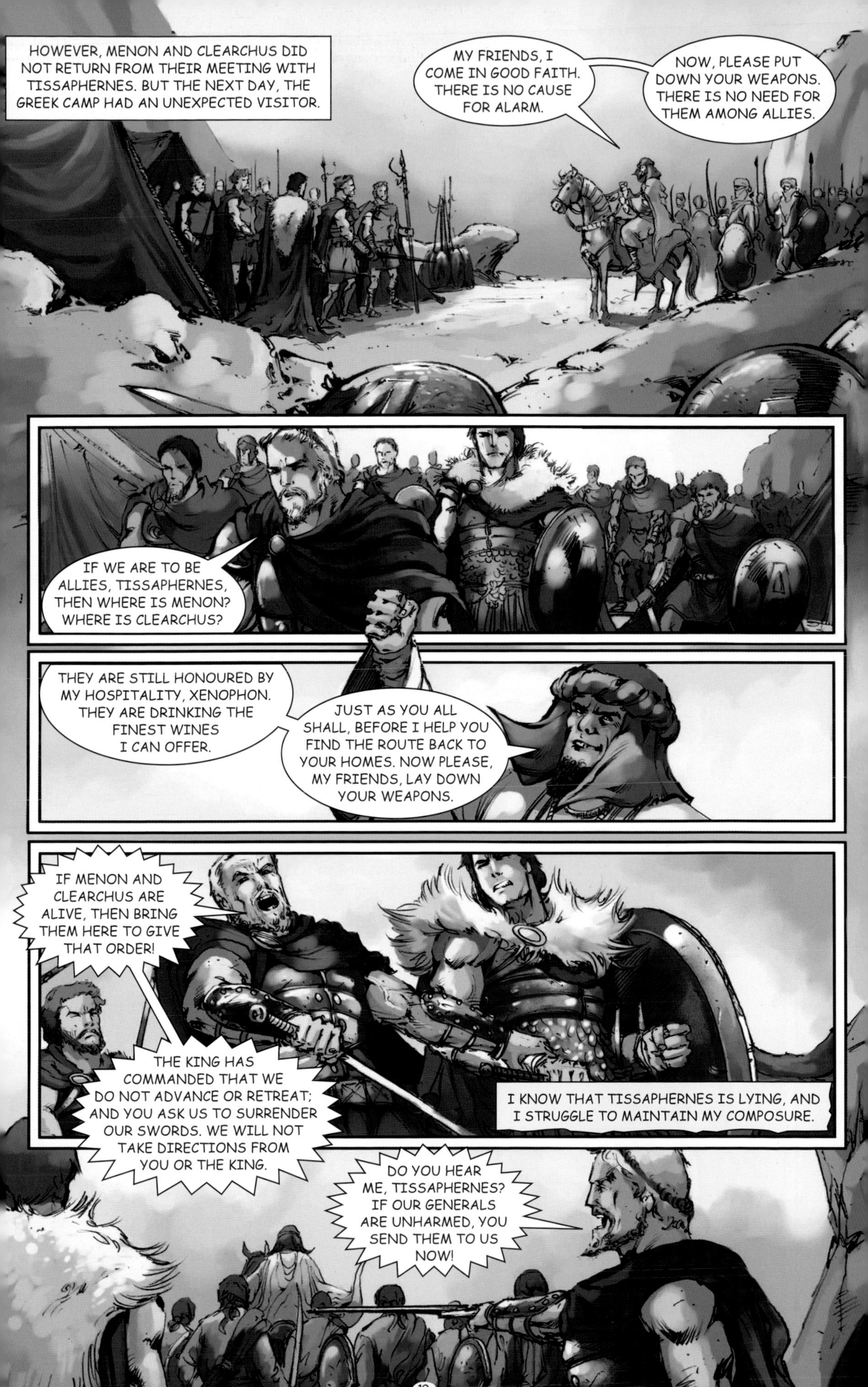
HOWEVER, MENON AND CLEARCHUS DID NOT RETURN FROM THEIR MEETING WITH TISSAPHERNES. BUT THE NEXT DAY, THE GREEK CAMP HAD AN UNEXPECTED VISITOR.
MY FRIENDS, I COME IN GOOD FAITH. THERE IS NO CAUSE FOR ALARM.
NOW, PLEASE PUT DOWN YOUR WEAPONS. THERE IS NO NEED FOR THEM AMONG ALLIES.
IF WE ARE TO BE ALLIES, TISSAPHERNES, THEN WHERE IS MENON? WHERE IS CLEARCHUS?
THEY ARE STILL HONOURED BY MY HOSPITALITY, XENOPHON. THEY ARE DRINKING THE FINEST WINES I CAN OFFER.
JUST AS YOU ALL SHALL, BEFORE I HELP YOU FIND THE ROUTE BACK TO YOUR HOMES. NOW PLEASE, MY FRIENDS, LAY DOWN YOUR WEAPONS.
IF MENON AND CLEARCHUS ARE ALIVE, THEN BRING THEM HERE TO GIVE THAT ORDER!
THE KING HAS COMMANDED THAT WE DO NOT ADVANCE OR RETREAT; AND YOU ASK US TO SURRENDER OUR SWORDS. WE WILL NOT TAKE DIRECTIONS FROM YOU OR THE KING.
I KNOW THAT TISSAPHERNES IS LYING, AND I STRUGGLE TO MAINTAIN MY COMPOSURE.
DO YOU HEAR ME, TISSAPHERNES? IF OUR GENERALS ARE UNHARMED, YOU SEND THEM TO US NOW!

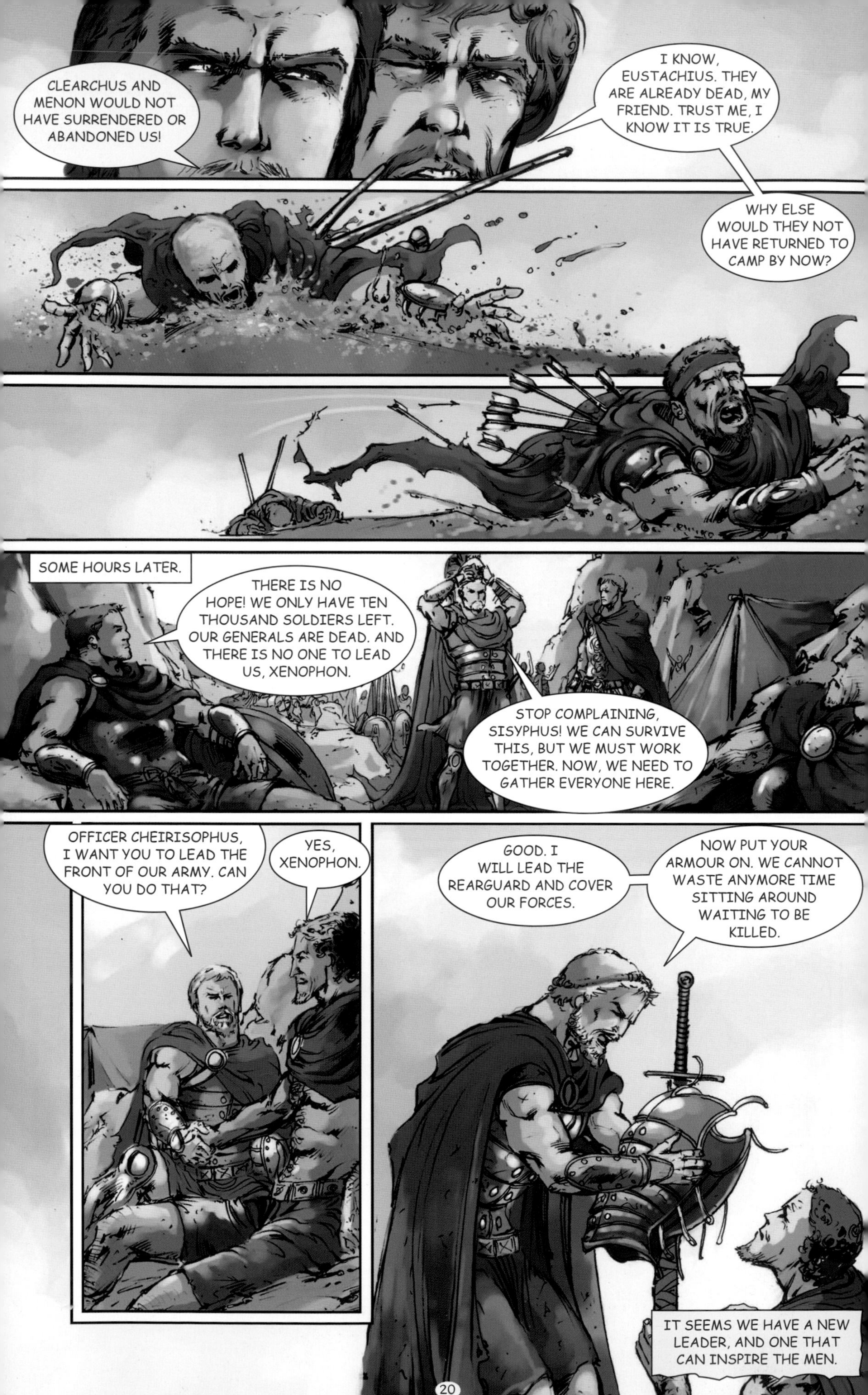
CLEARCHUS AND MENON WOULD NOT HAVE SURRENDERED OR ABANDONED US!
I KNOW, EUSTACHIUS. THEY ARE ALREADY DEAD, MY FRIEND. TRUST ME, I KNOW IT IS TRUE.
WHY ELSE WOULD THEY NOT HAVE RETURNED TO CAMP BY NOW?
SOME HOURS LATER.
THERE IS NO HOPE! WE ONLY HAVE TEN THOUSAND SOLDIERS LEFT. OUR GENERALS ARE DEAD. AND THERE IS NO ONE TO LEAD US, XENOPHON.
STOP COMPLAINING, SISYPHUS! WE CAN SURVIVE THIS, BUT WE MUST WORK TOGETHER. NOW, WE NEED TO GATHER EVERYONE HERE.
OFFICER CHEIRISOPHUS, I WANT YOU TO LEAD THE FRONT OF OUR ARMY. CAN YOU DO THAT?
YES, XENOPHON.
GOOD. I WILL LEAD THE REARGUARD AND COVER OUR FORCES.
NOW PUT YOUR ARMOUR ON. WE CANNOT WASTE ANYMORE TIME SITTING AROUND WAITING TO BE KILLED.
IT SEEMS WE HAVE A NEW LEADER, AND ONE THAT CAN INSPIRE THE MEN.

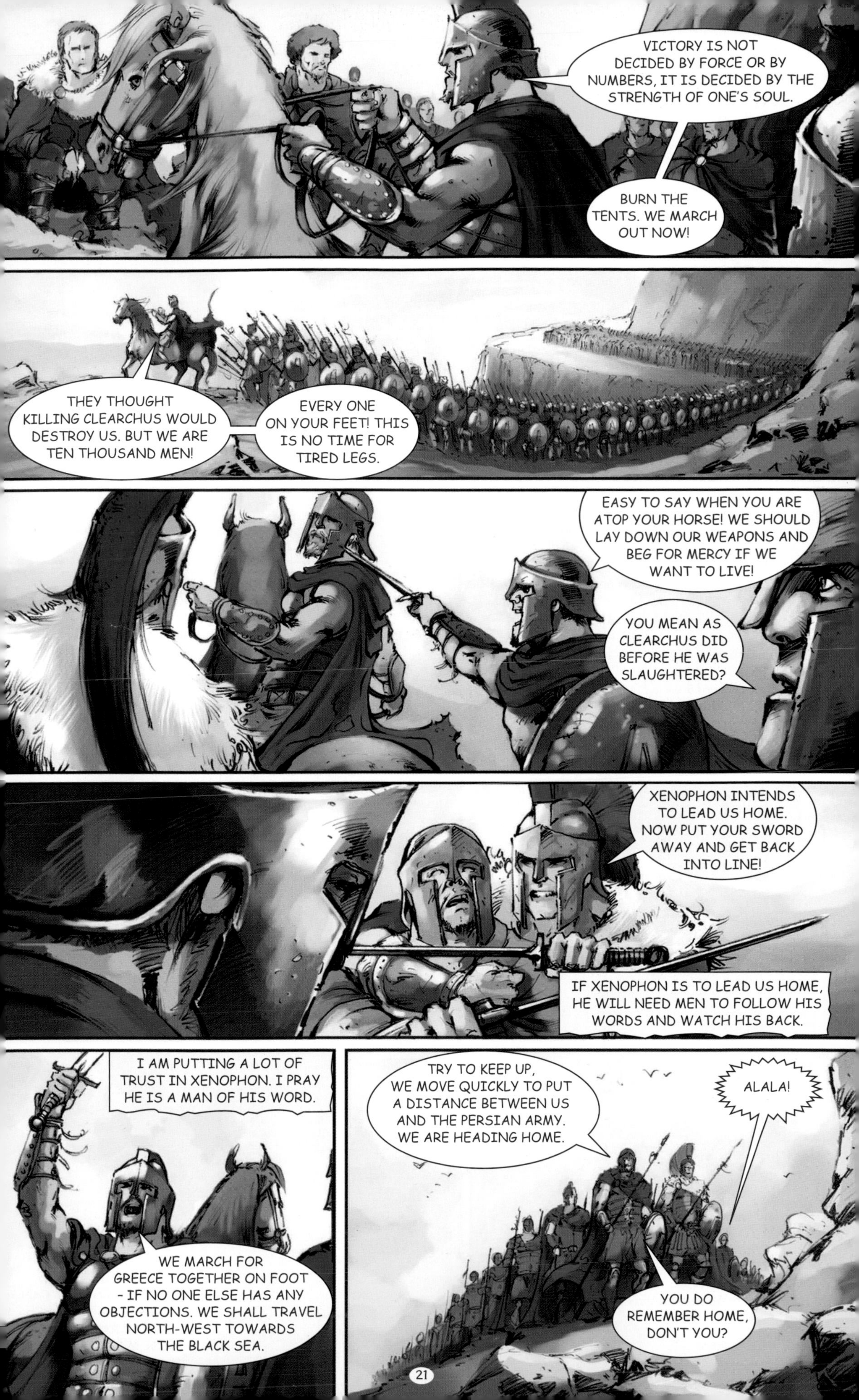
VICTORY IS NOT DECIDED BY FORCE OR BY NUMBERS, IT IS DECIDED BY THE STRENGTH OF ONE'S SOUL.
BURN THE TENTS. WE MARCH OUT NOW!
THEY THOUGHT KILLING CLEARCHUS WOULD DESTROY US. BUT WE ARE TEN THOUSAND MEN!
EVERY ONE ON YOUR FEET! THIS IS NO TIME FOR TIRED LEGS.
EASY TO SAY WHEN YOU ARE ATOP YOUR HORSE! WE SHOULD LAY DOWN OUR WEAPONS AND BEG FOR MERCY IF WE WANT TO LIVE!
YOU MEAN AS CLEARCHUS DID BEFORE HE WAS SLAUGHTERED?
XENOPHON INTENDS TO LEAD US HOME. NOW PUT YOUR SWORD AWAY AND GET BACK INTO LINE!
IF XENOPHON IS TO LEAD US HOME, HE WILL NEED MEN TO FOLLOW HIS WORDS AND WATCH HIS BACK.
I AM PUTTING A LOT OF TRUST IN XENOPHON. I PRAY HE IS A MAN OF HIS WORD.
WE MARCH FOR GREECE TOGETHER ON FOOT - IF NO ONE ELSE HAS ANY OBJECTIONS. WE SHALL TRAVEL NORTH-WEST TOWARDS THE BLACK SEA.
TRY TO KEEP UP, WE MOVE QUICKLY TO PUT A DISTANCE BETWEEN US AND THE PERSIAN ARMY. WE ARE HEADING HOME.
ALALA!
YOU DO REMEMBER HOME, DON'T YOU?

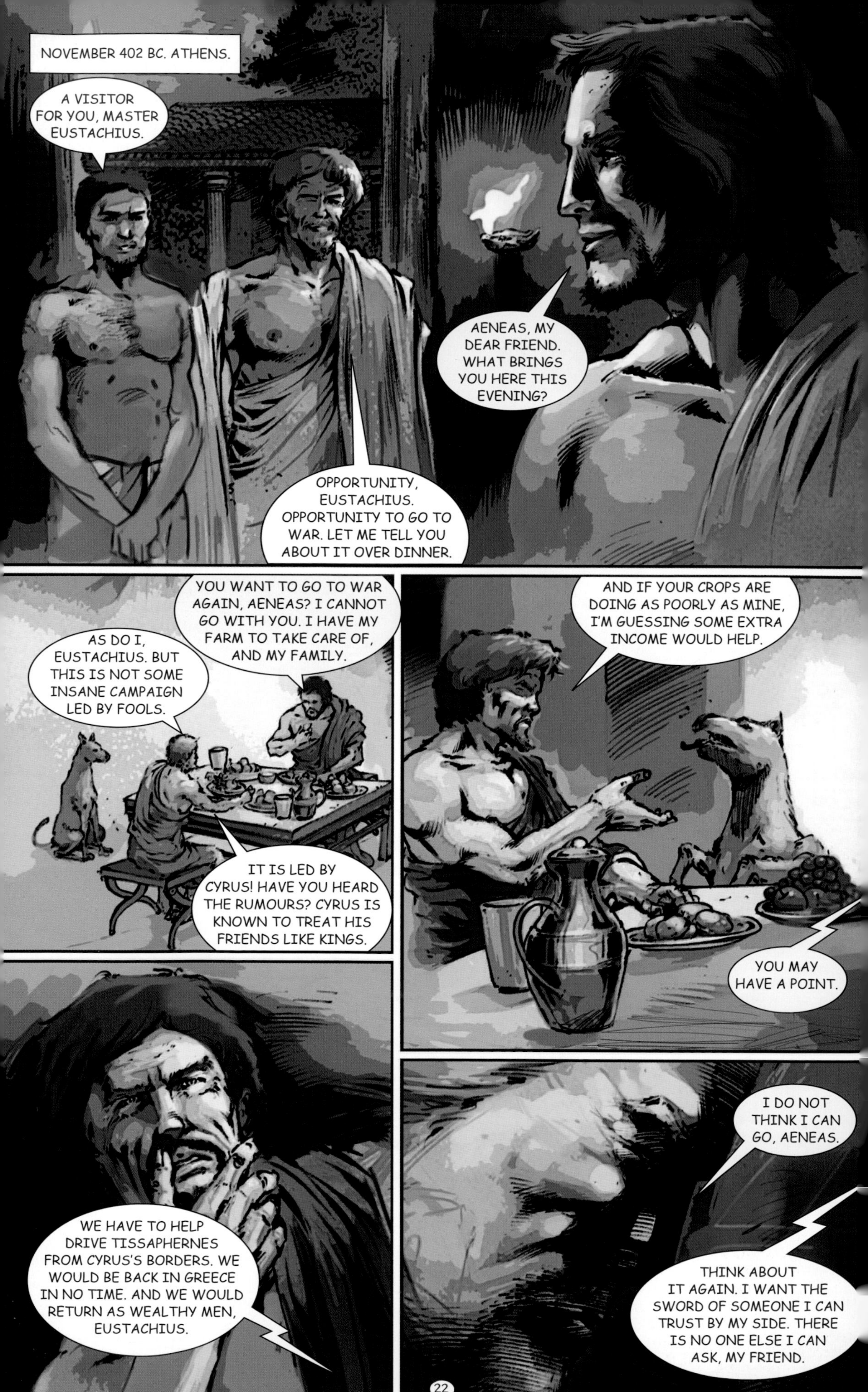

NOVEMBER 402 BC. ATHENS.
A VISITOR FOR YOU, MASTER EUSTACHIUS.
AENEAS, MY DEAR FRIEND. WHAT BRINGS YOU HERE THIS EVENING?
OPPORTUNITY, EUSTACHIUS. OPPORTUNITY TO GO TO WAR. LET ME TELL YOU ABOUT IT OVER DINNER.
YOU WANT TO GO TO WAR AGAIN, AENEAS? I CANNOT GO WITH YOU. I HAVE MY FARM TO TAKE CARE OF, AND MY FAMILY.
AS DO I, EUSTACHIUS. BUT THIS IS NOT SOME INSANE CAMPAIGN LED BY FOOLS.
IT IS LED BY CYRUS! HAVE YOU HEARD THE RUMOURS? CYRUS IS KNOWN TO TREAT HIS FRIENDS LIKE KINGS.
AND IF YOUR CROPS ARE DOING AS POORLY AS MINE, I'M GUESSING SOME EXTRA INCOME WOULD HELP.
YOU MAY HAVE A POINT.
WE HAVE TO HELP DRIVE TISSAPHERNES FROM CYRUS'S BORDERS. WE WOULD BE BACK IN GREECE IN NO TIME. AND WE WOULD RETURN AS WEALTHY MEN, EUSTACHIUS.
I DO NOT THINK I CAN GO, AENEAS.
THINK ABOUT IT AGAIN. I WANT THE SWORD OF SOMEONE I CAN TRUST BY MY SIDE. THERE IS NO ONE ELSE I CAN ASK, MY FRIEND.

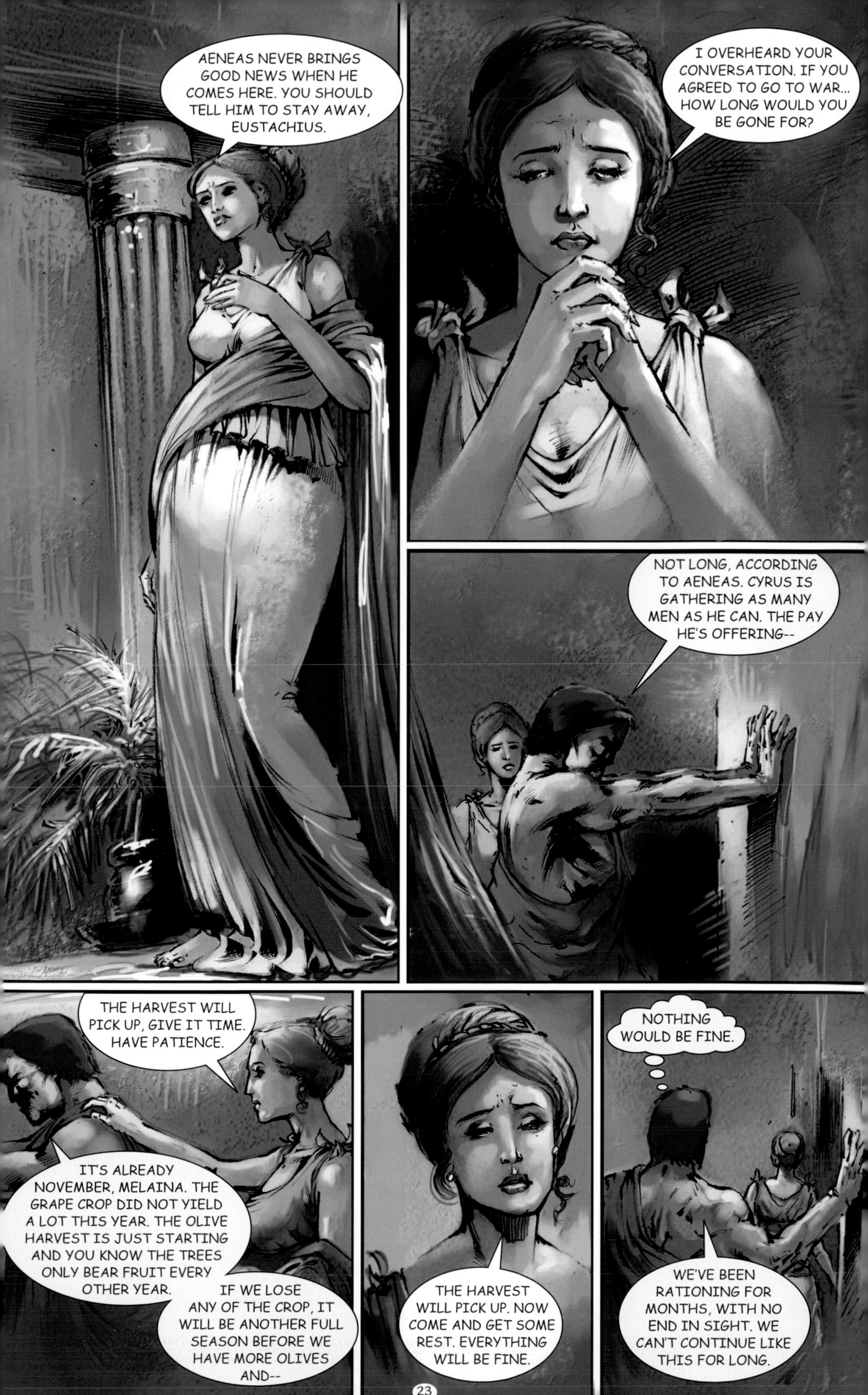
AENEAS NEVER BRINGS GOOD NEWS WHEN HE COMES HERE. YOU SHOULD TELL HIM TO STAY AWAY, EUSTACHIUS.
I OVERHEARD YOUR CONVERSATION. IF YOU AGREED TO GO TO WAR... HOW LONG WOULD YOU BE GONE FOR?
NOT LONG, ACCORDING TO AENEAS. CYRUS IS GATHERING AS MANY MEN AS HE CAN. THE PAY HE'S OFFERING--
THE HARVEST WILL PICK UP, GIVE IT TIME. HAVE PATIENCE.
IT'S ALREADY NOVEMBER, MELAINA. THE GRAPE CROP DID NOT YIELD A LOT THIS YEAR. THE OLIVE HARVEST IS JUST STARTING AND YOU KNOW THE TREES ONLY BEAR FRUIT EVERY OTHER YEAR.
IF WE LOSE ANY OF THE CROP, IT WILL BE ANOTHER FULL SEASON BEFORE WE HAVE MORE OLIVES AND--
THE HARVEST WILL PICK UP. NOW COME AND GET SOME REST. EVERYTHING WILL BE FINE.
NOTHING WOULD BE FINE.
WE'VE BEEN RATIONING FOR MONTHS, WITH NO END IN SIGHT. WE CAN'T CONTINUE LIKE THIS FOR LONG.

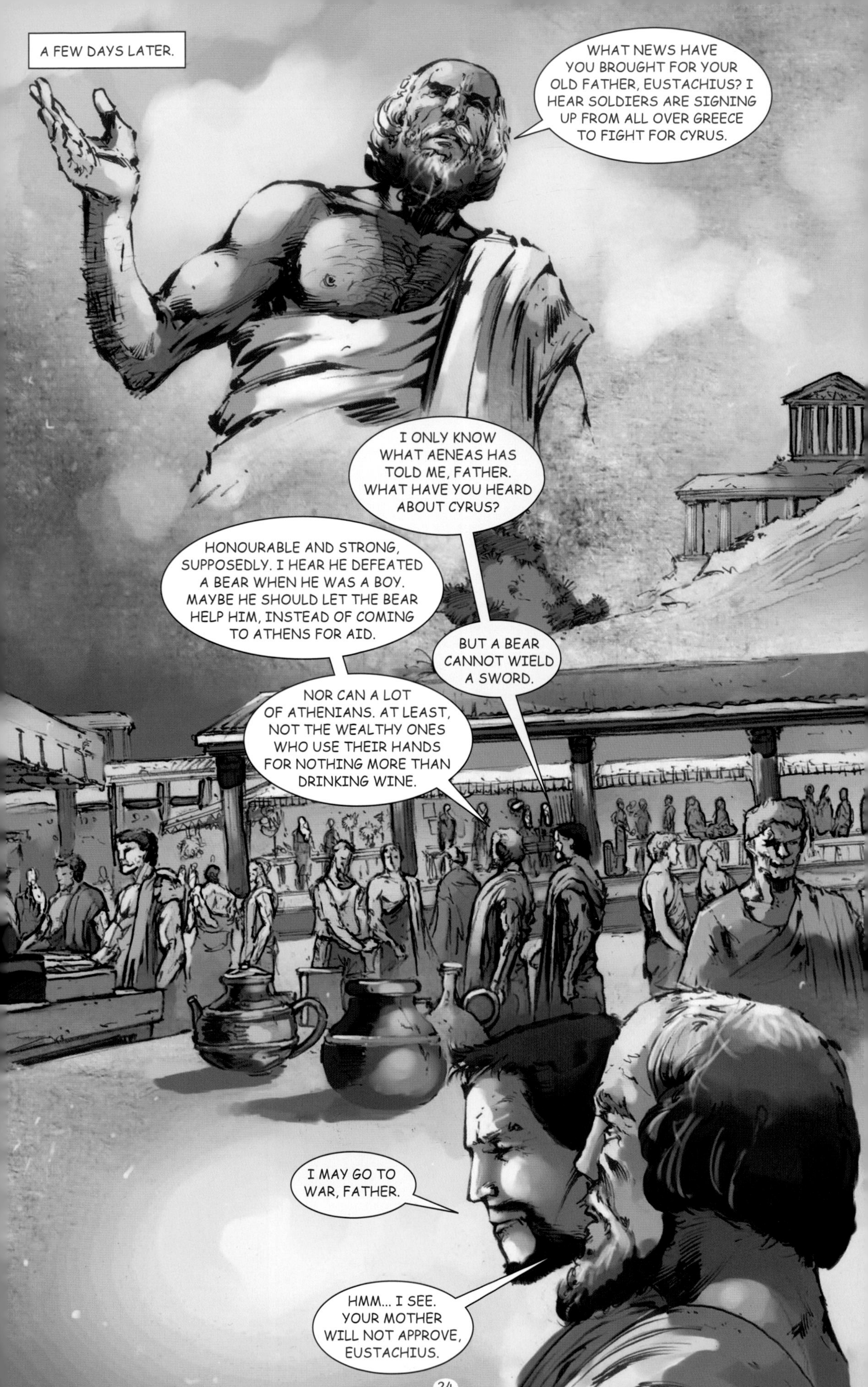
A FEW DAYS LATER.
WHAT NEWS HAVE YOU BROUGHT FOR YOUR OLD FATHER, EUSTACHIUS? I HEAR SOLDIERS ARE SIGNING UP FROM ALL OVER GREECE TO FIGHT FOR CYRUS.
I ONLY KNOW WHAT AENEAS HAS TOLD ME, FATHER. WHAT HAVE YOU HEARD ABOUT CYRUS?
HONOURABLE AND STRONG, SUPPOSEDLY. I HEAR HE DEFEATED A BEAR WHEN HE WAS A BOY. MAYBE HE SHOULD LET THE BEAR HELP HIM, INSTEAD OF COMING TO ATHENS FOR AID.
BUT A BEAR CANNOT WIELD A SWORD.
NOR CAN A LOT OF ATHENIANS. AT LEAST, NOT THE WEALTHY ONES WHO USE THEIR HANDS FOR NOTHING MORE THAN DRINKING WINE.
I MAY GO TO WAR, FATHER.
HMM... I SEE. YOUR MOTHER WILL NOT APPROVE, EUSTACHIUS.

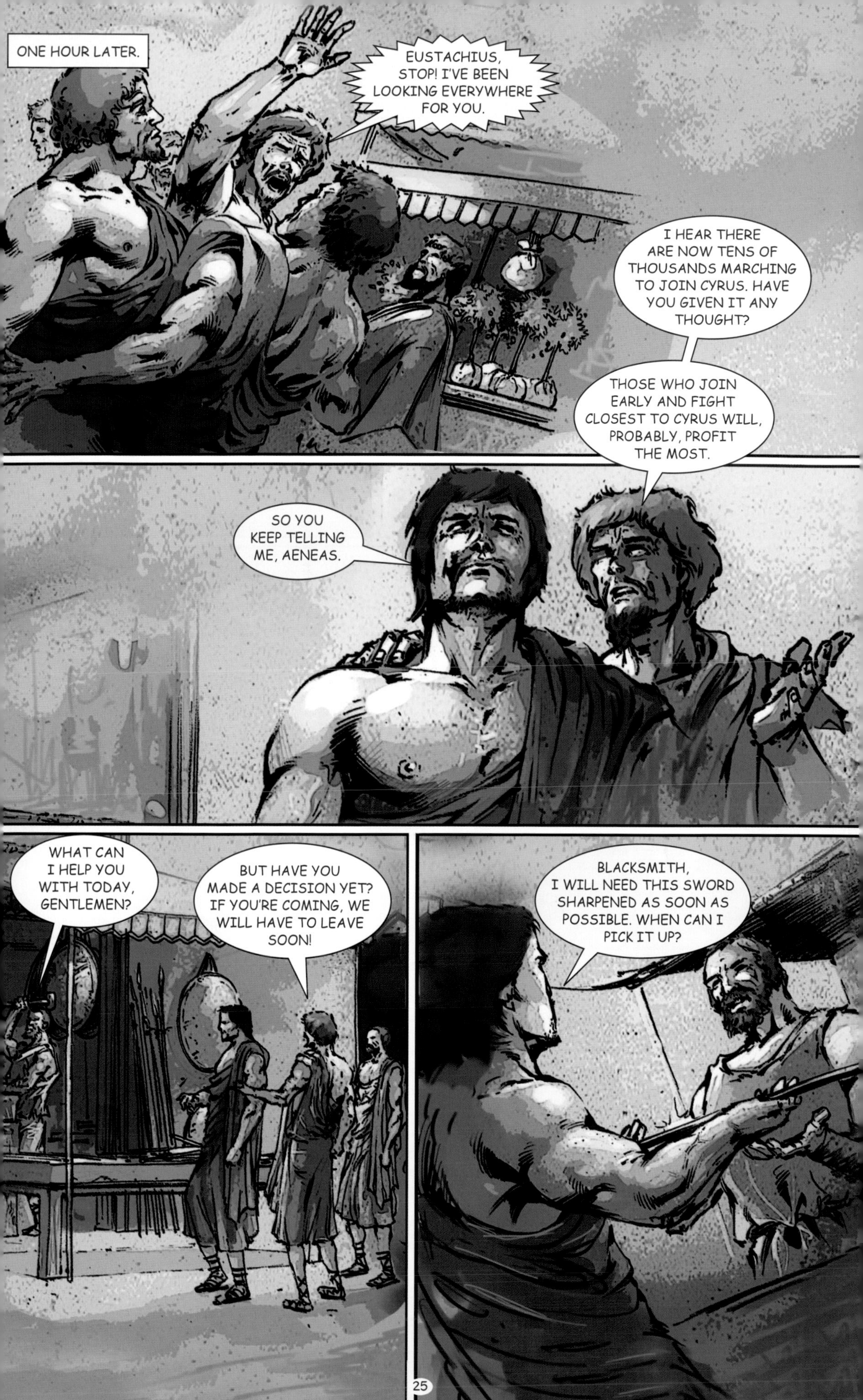
ONE HOUR LATER.
EUSTACHIUS, STOP! I'VE BEEN LOOKING EVERYWHERE FOR YOU.
I HEAR THERE ARE NOW TENS OF THOUSANDS MARCHING TO JOIN CYRUS. HAVE YOU GIVEN IT ANY THOUGHT?
THOSE WHO JOIN EARLY AND FIGHT CLOSEST TO CYRUS WILL, PROBABLY, PROFIT THE MOST.
SO YOU KEEP TELLING ME, AENEAS.
WHAT CAN I HELP YOU WITH TODAY, GENTLEMEN?
BUT HAVE YOU MADE A DECISION YET? IF YOU'RE COMING, WE WILL HAVE TO LEAVE SOON!
BLACKSMITH, I WILL NEED THIS SWORD SHARPENED AS SOON AS POSSIBLE. WHEN CAN I PICK IT UP?

TWO DAYS LATER.

AH, MASTER EUSTACHIUS, IS IT TRUE YOU ARE LEAVING FOR WAR?

IT IS, GREGORIOS. BUT AT THE RATE THAT MULE IS MOVING, I SHOULD BE BACK BEFORE THAT OIL IS PRESSED. HOW ARE THE GROVES HOLDING UP?

IF THEY CAN HOLD ON IN THIS SOIL, THERE SHOULD BE A DECENT HARVEST BY FEBRUARY. BUT IF NOT--

IF NOT, THERE WILL BE NO PROFIT THIS SEASON OR NEXT.

THAT MAY COME TO PASS, MASTER. WE BEG THE ALMIGHTY ZEUS FOR RAIN, BUT RECEIVE NO ANSWER.

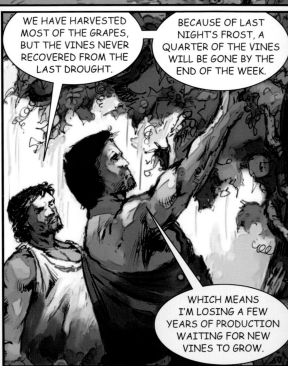

WE HAVE HARVESTED MOST OF THE GRAPES, BUT THE VINES NEVER RECOVERED FROM THE LAST DROUGHT.

BECAUSE OF LAST NIGHT'S FROST, A QUARTER OF THE VINES WILL BE GONE BY THE END OF THE WEEK.

WHICH MEANS I'M LOSING A FEW YEARS OF PRODUCTION WAITING FOR NEW VINES TO GROW.

CONTACT MY FATHER IF THINGS BECOME WORSE, GREGORIOS.

26

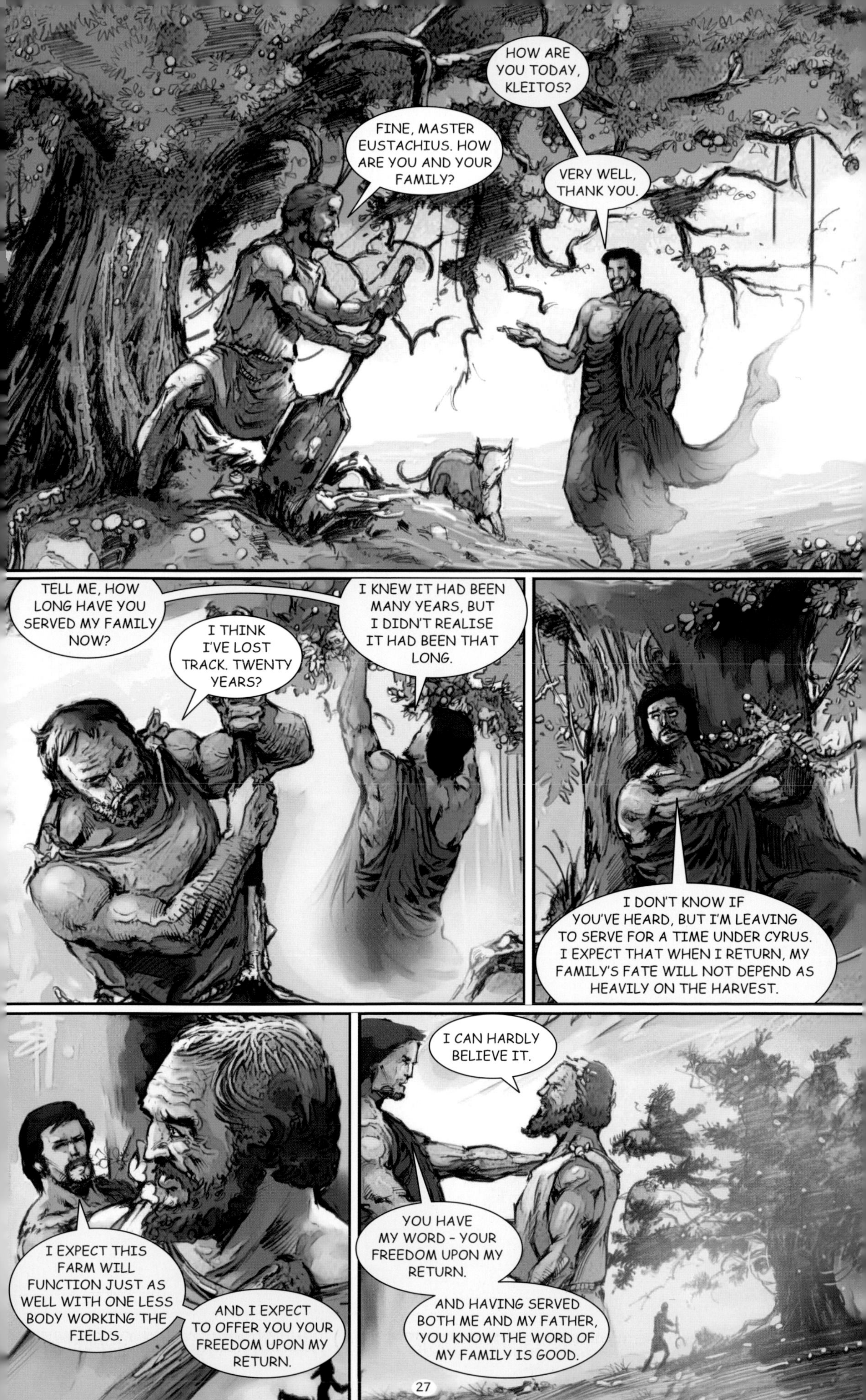
HOW ARE YOU TODAY, KLEITOS?
FINE, MASTER EUSTACHIUS. HOW ARE YOU AND YOUR FAMILY?
VERY WELL, THANK YOU.
TELL ME, HOW LONG HAVE YOU SERVED MY FAMILY NOW?
I THINK I'VE LOST TRACK. TWENTY YEARS?
I KNEW IT HAD BEEN MANY YEARS, BUT I DIDN'T REALISE IT HAD BEEN THAT LONG.
I DON'T KNOW IF YOU'VE HEARD, BUT I'M LEAVING TO SERVE FOR A TIME UNDER CYRUS. I EXPECT THAT WHEN I RETURN, MY FAMILY'S FATE WILL NOT DEPEND AS HEAVILY ON THE HARVEST.
I EXPECT THIS FARM WILL FUNCTION JUST AS WELL WITH ONE LESS BODY WORKING THE FIELDS.
AND I EXPECT TO OFFER YOU YOUR FREEDOM UPON MY RETURN.
I CAN HARDLY BELIEVE IT.
YOU HAVE MY WORD – YOUR FREEDOM UPON MY RETURN.
AND HAVING SERVED BOTH ME AND MY FATHER, YOU KNOW THE WORD OF MY FAMILY IS GOOD.

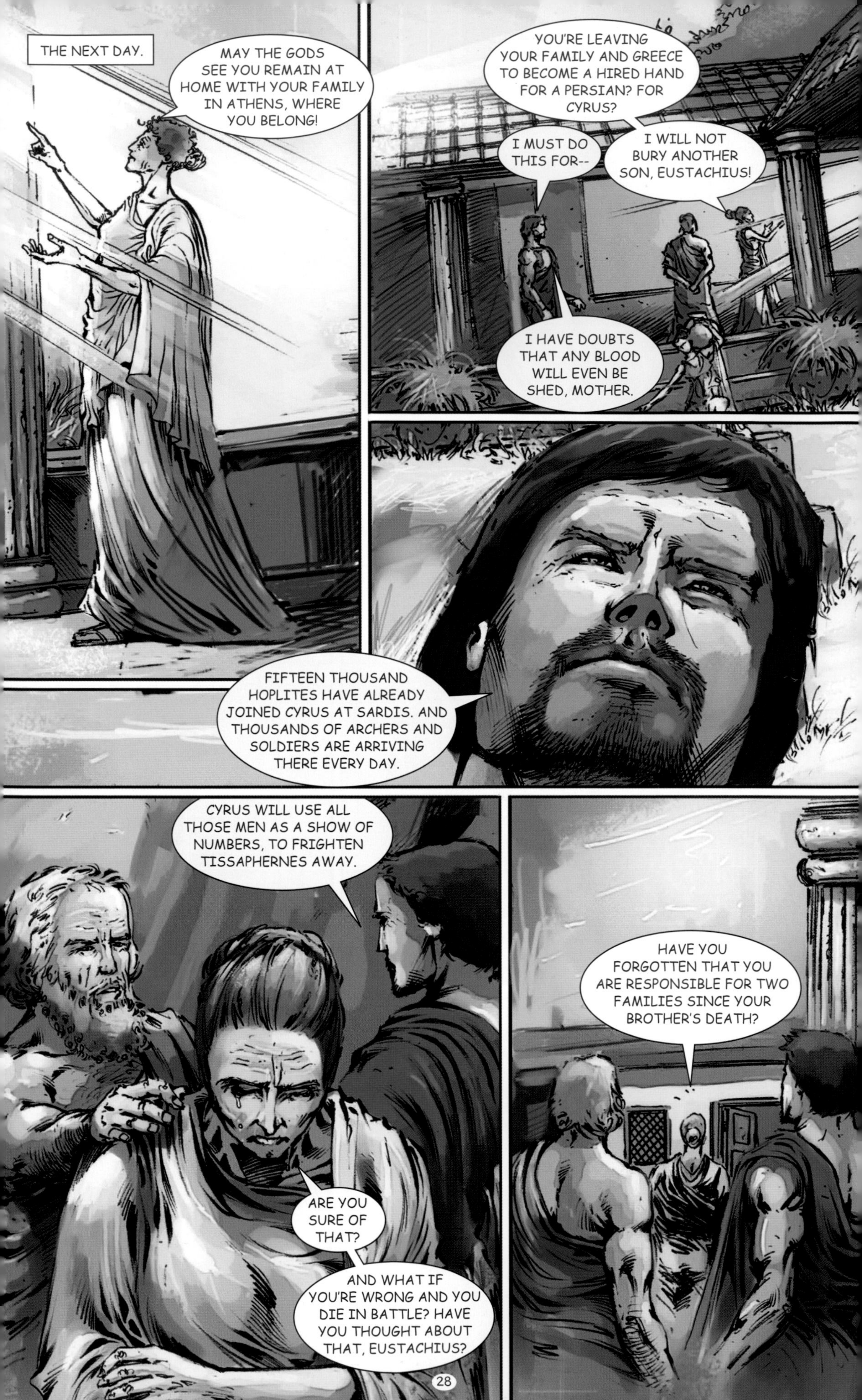
THE NEXT DAY.
MAY THE GODS SEE YOU REMAIN AT HOME WITH YOUR FAMILY IN ATHENS, WHERE YOU BELONG!
YOU'RE LEAVING YOUR FAMILY AND GREECE TO BECOME A HIRED HAND FOR A PERSIAN? FOR CYRUS?
I MUST DO THIS FOR--
I WILL NOT BURY ANOTHER SON, EUSTACHIUS!
I HAVE DOUBTS THAT ANY BLOOD WILL EVEN BE SHED, MOTHER.
FIFTEEN THOUSAND HOPLITES HAVE ALREADY JOINED CYRUS AT SARDIS. AND THOUSANDS OF ARCHERS AND SOLDIERS ARE ARRIVING THERE EVERY DAY.
CYRUS WILL USE ALL THOSE MEN AS A SHOW OF NUMBERS, TO FRIGHTEN TISSAPHERNES AWAY.
ARE YOU SURE OF THAT?
AND WHAT IF YOU'RE WRONG AND YOU DIE IN BATTLE? HAVE YOU THOUGHT ABOUT THAT, EUSTACHIUS?
HAVE YOU FORGOTTEN THAT YOU ARE RESPONSIBLE FOR TWO FAMILIES SINCE YOUR BROTHER'S DEATH?

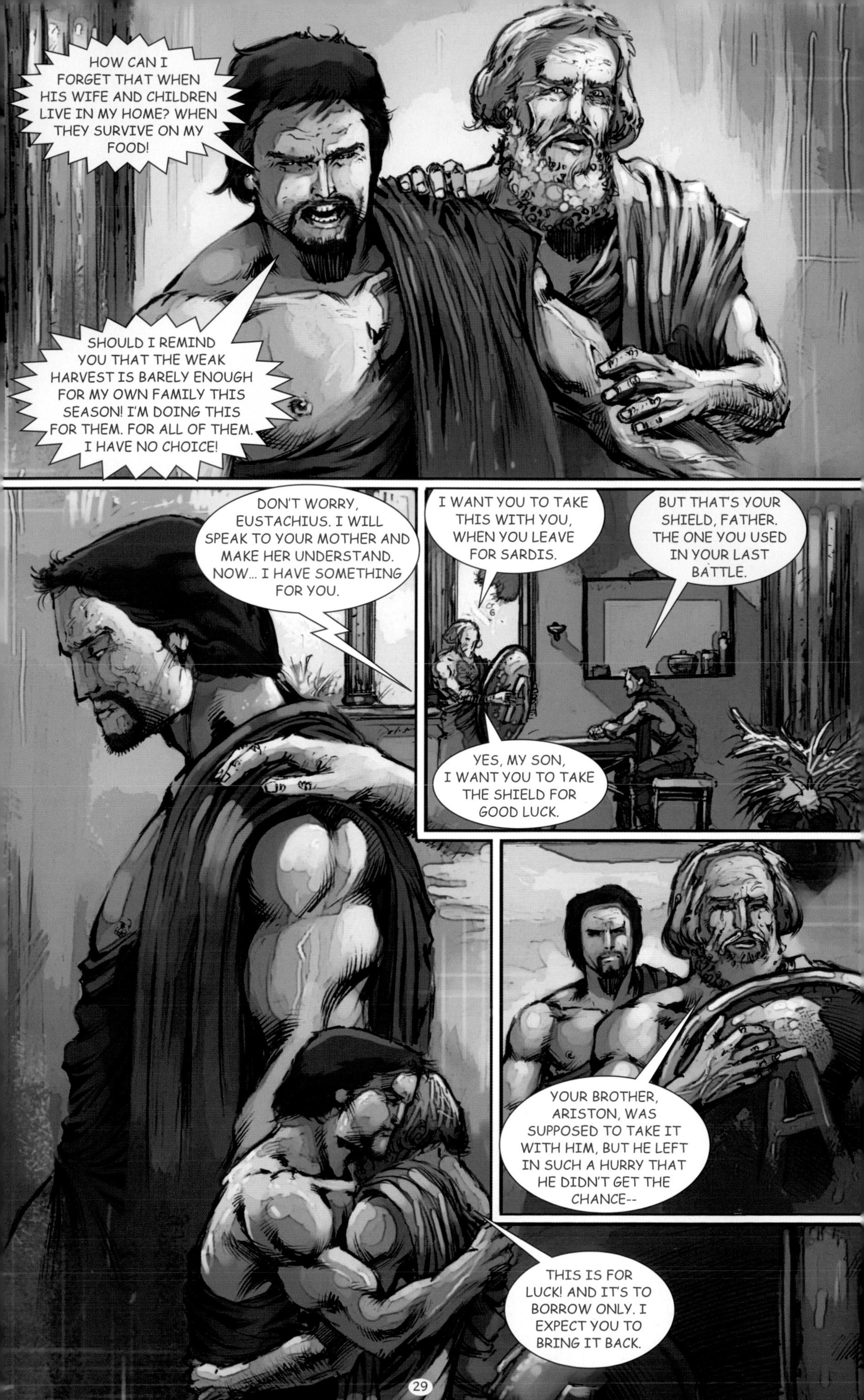
HOW CAN I FORGET THAT WHEN HIS WIFE AND CHILDREN LIVE IN MY HOME? WHEN THEY SURVIVE ON MY FOOD!
SHOULD I REMIND YOU THAT THE WEAK HARVEST IS BARELY ENOUGH FOR MY OWN FAMILY THIS SEASON! I'M DOING THIS FOR THEM. FOR ALL OF THEM. I HAVE NO CHOICE!
DON'T WORRY, EUSTACHIUS. I WILL SPEAK TO YOUR MOTHER AND MAKE HER UNDERSTAND. NOW... I HAVE SOMETHING FOR YOU.
I WANT YOU TO TAKE THIS WITH YOU, WHEN YOU LEAVE FOR SARDIS.
BUT THAT'S YOUR SHIELD, FATHER. THE ONE YOU USED IN YOUR LAST BATTLE.
YES, MY SON, I WANT YOU TO TAKE THE SHIELD FOR GOOD LUCK.
YOUR BROTHER, ARISTON, WAS SUPPOSED TO TAKE IT WITH HIM, BUT HE LEFT IN SUCH A HURRY THAT HE DIDN'T GET THE CHANCE--
THIS IS FOR LUCK! AND IT'S TO BORROW ONLY. I EXPECT YOU TO BRING IT BACK.

THUD!

HOW LONG HAVE WE BEEN WAITING HERE? I THOUGHT YOU PROMISED THIS CAMPAIGN WOULD BE QUICK AND EASY, AENEAS.

I'M BEGINNING TO QUESTION THAT PROMISE NOW. I FEEL LIKE I'VE BEEN FIGHTING HERE FOR CENTURIES!

THWACK!

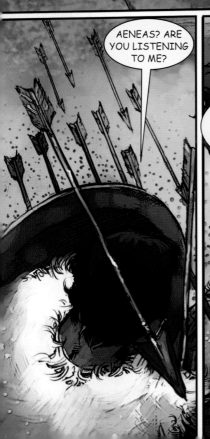

AENEAS? ARE YOU LISTENING TO ME?

WHERE IS THE ARMY? WHO ARE YOU? I DEMAND TO KNOW WHAT IS HAPPENING? WHAT IS THIS MADNESS?

THIS IS THE CALM BEFORE THE STORM, EUSTACHIUS. RUN AWAY WHILE YOU STILL CAN.

I AM A WARRIOR OF ATHENS. EVEN IF MY FRIENDS HAVE BEEN TAKEN BY WHATEVER DARKNESS LURKS IN THOSE WOODS, I WILL NOT RUN. I WILL NOT--

YOUR FRIENDS ARE GONE AND YOU DIE NEXT, EUSTACHIUS!

HA HA HA!

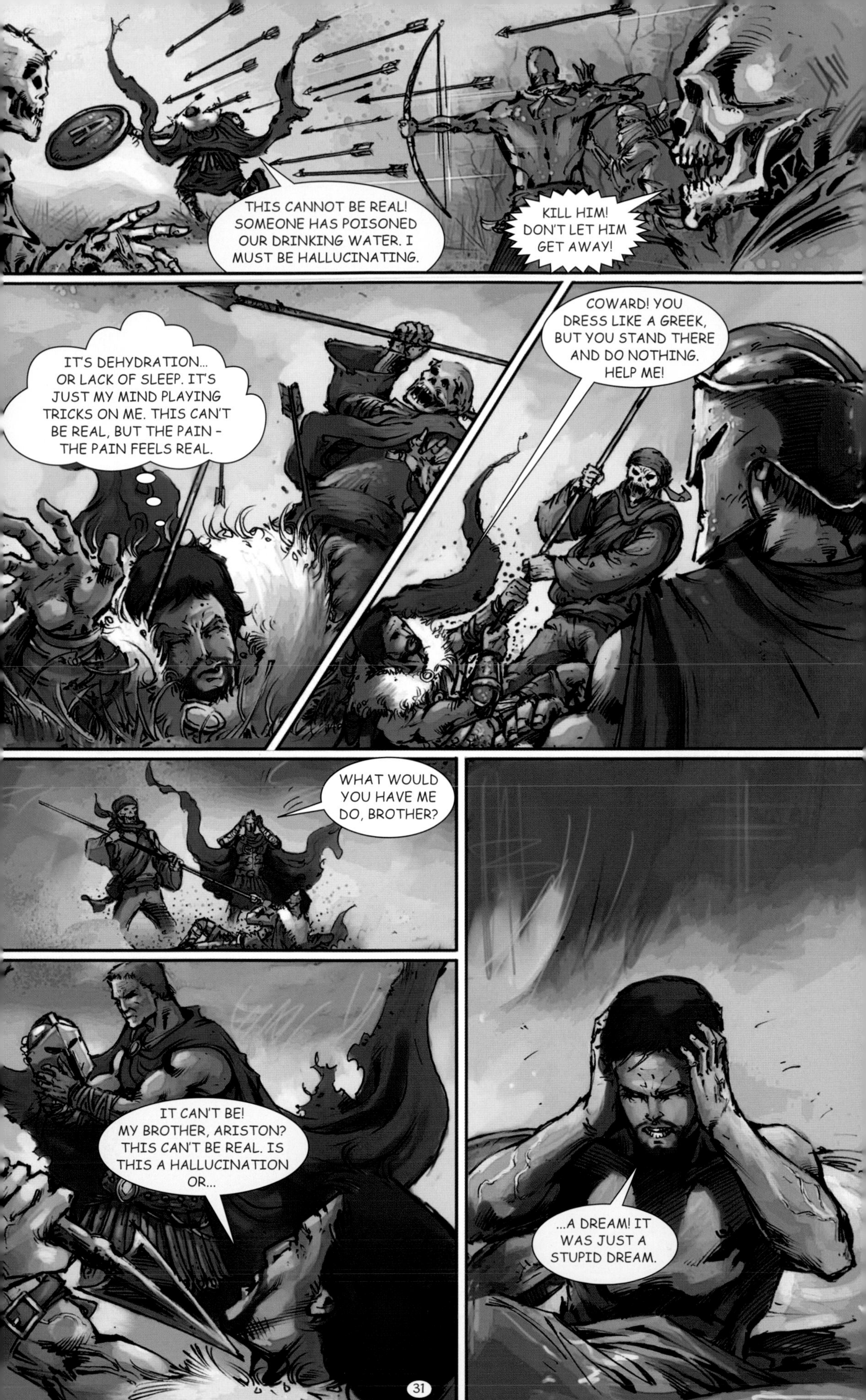
THIS CANNOT BE REAL! SOMEONE HAS POISONED OUR DRINKING WATER. I MUST BE HALLUCINATING.
KILL HIM! DON'T LET HIM GET AWAY!
IT'S DEHYDRATION... OR LACK OF SLEEP. IT'S JUST MY MIND PLAYING TRICKS ON ME. THIS CAN'T BE REAL, BUT THE PAIN – THE PAIN FEELS REAL.
COWARD! YOU DRESS LIKE A GREEK, BUT YOU STAND THERE AND DO NOTHING. HELP ME!
WHAT WOULD YOU HAVE ME DO, BROTHER?
IT CAN'T BE! MY BROTHER, ARISTON? THIS CAN'T BE REAL. IS THIS A HALLUCINATION OR...
...A DREAM! IT WAS JUST A STUPID DREAM.

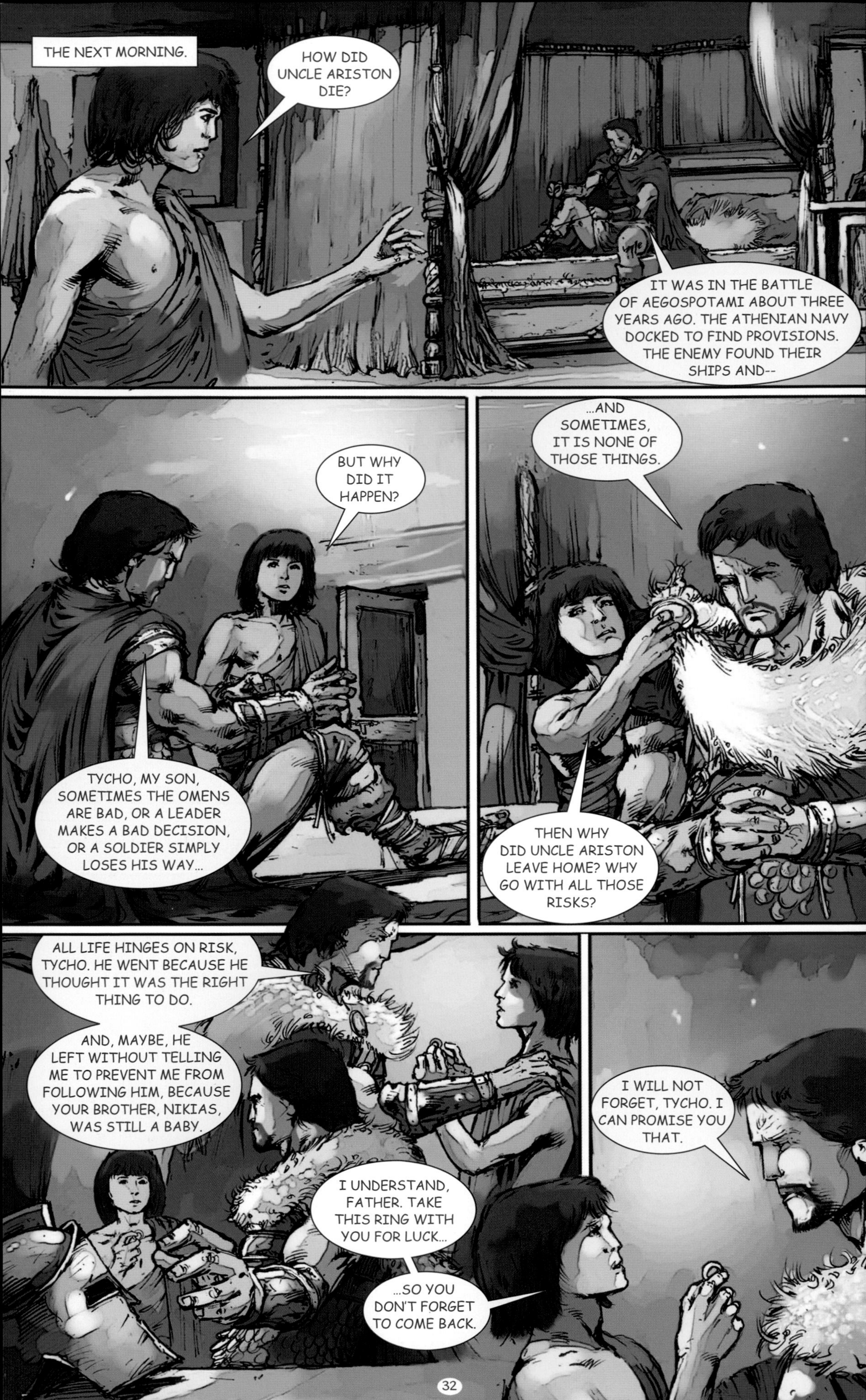
THE NEXT MORNING.
HOW DID UNCLE ARISTON DIE?
IT WAS IN THE BATTLE OF AEGOSPOTAMI ABOUT THREE YEARS AGO. THE ATHENIAN NAVY DOCKED TO FIND PROVISIONS. THE ENEMY FOUND THEIR SHIPS AND--
BUT WHY DID IT HAPPEN?
TYCHO, MY SON, SOMETIMES THE OMENS ARE BAD, OR A LEADER MAKES A BAD DECISION, OR A SOLDIER SIMPLY LOSES HIS WAY...
...AND SOMETIMES, IT IS NONE OF THOSE THINGS.
THEN WHY DID UNCLE ARISTON LEAVE HOME? WHY GO WITH ALL THOSE RISKS?
ALL LIFE HINGES ON RISK, TYCHO. HE WENT BECAUSE HE THOUGHT IT WAS THE RIGHT THING TO DO.
AND, MAYBE, HE LEFT WITHOUT TELLING ME TO PREVENT ME FROM FOLLOWING HIM, BECAUSE YOUR BROTHER, NIKIAS, WAS STILL A BABY.
I UNDERSTAND, FATHER. TAKE THIS RING WITH YOU FOR LUCK...
...SO YOU DON'T FORGET TO COME BACK.
I WILL NOT FORGET, TYCHO. I CAN PROMISE YOU THAT.

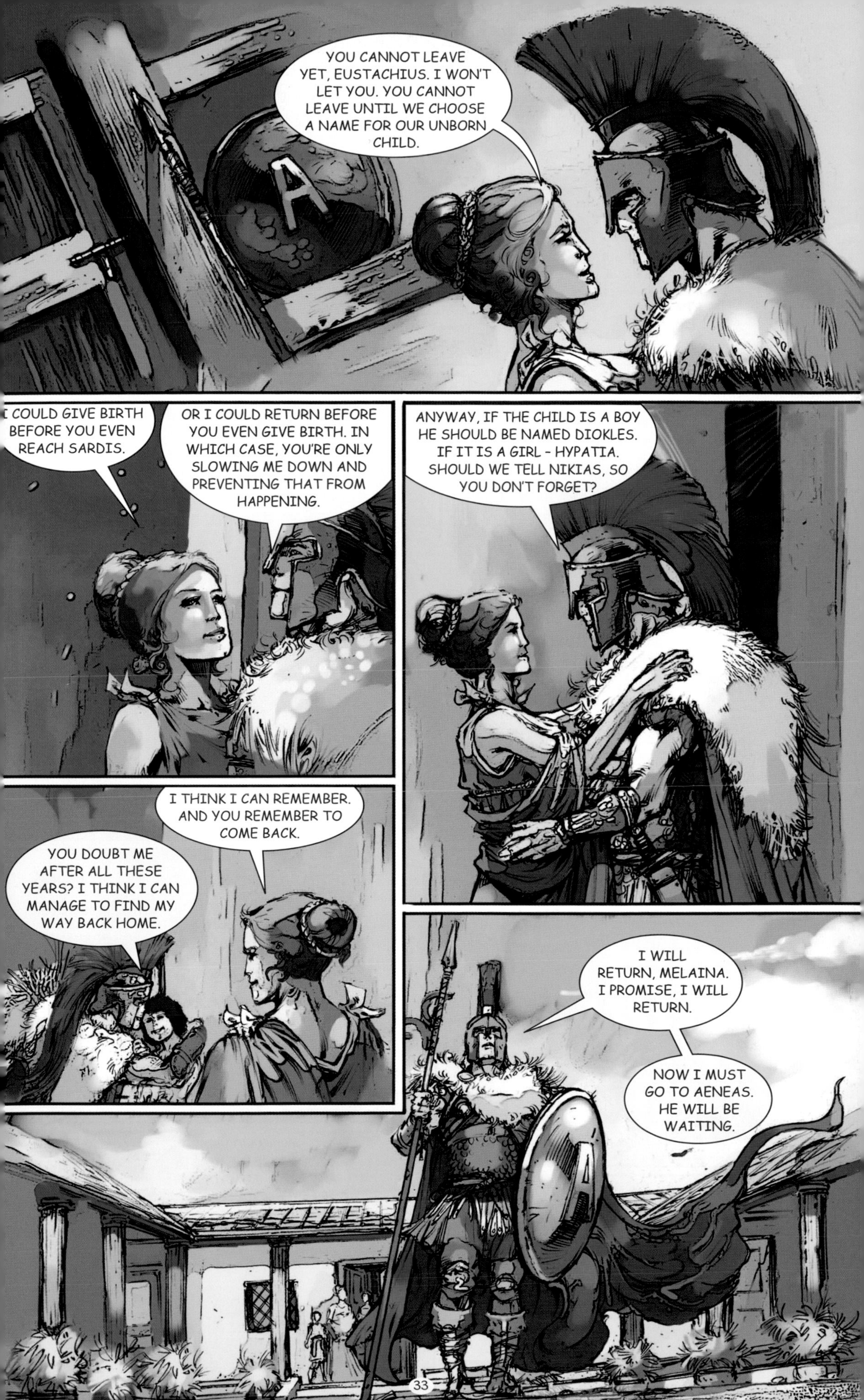
YOU CANNOT LEAVE YET, EUSTACHIUS. I WON'T LET YOU. YOU CANNOT LEAVE UNTIL WE CHOOSE A NAME FOR OUR UNBORN CHILD.
I COULD GIVE BIRTH BEFORE YOU EVEN REACH SARDIS.
OR I COULD RETURN BEFORE YOU EVEN GIVE BIRTH. IN WHICH CASE, YOU'RE ONLY SLOWING ME DOWN AND PREVENTING THAT FROM HAPPENING.
ANYWAY, IF THE CHILD IS A BOY HE SHOULD BE NAMED DIOKLES. IF IT IS A GIRL - HYPATIA. SHOULD WE TELL NIKIAS, SO YOU DON'T FORGET?
I THINK I CAN REMEMBER. AND YOU REMEMBER TO COME BACK.
YOU DOUBT ME AFTER ALL THESE YEARS? I THINK I CAN MANAGE TO FIND MY WAY BACK HOME.
I WILL RETURN, MELAINA. I PROMISE, I WILL RETURN.
NOW I MUST GO TO AENEAS. HE WILL BE WAITING.

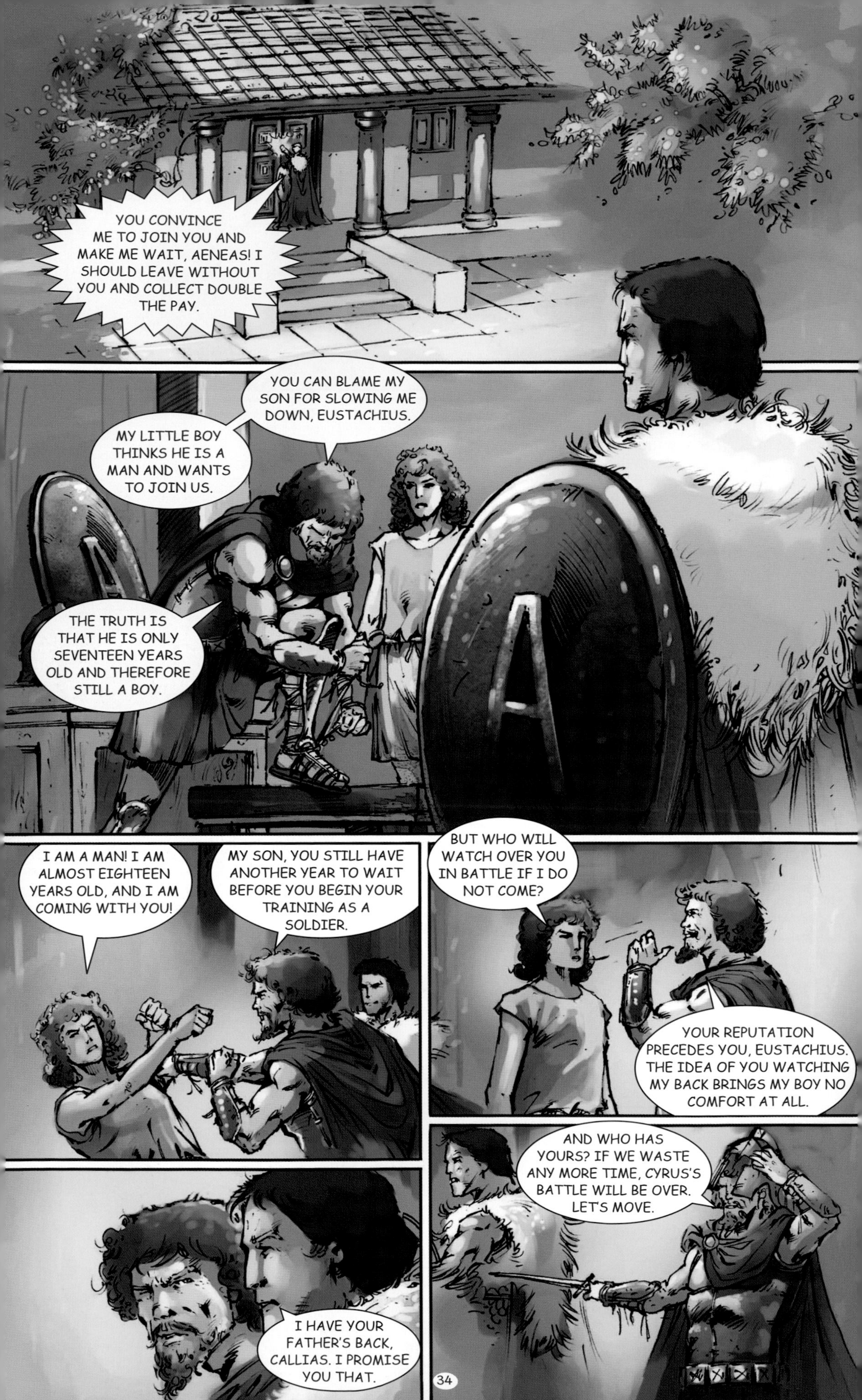
YOU CONVINCE ME TO JOIN YOU AND MAKE ME WAIT, AENEAS! I SHOULD LEAVE WITHOUT YOU AND COLLECT DOUBLE THE PAY.
YOU CAN BLAME MY SON FOR SLOWING ME DOWN, EUSTACHIUS.
MY LITTLE BOY THINKS HE IS A MAN AND WANTS TO JOIN US.
THE TRUTH IS THAT HE IS ONLY SEVENTEEN YEARS OLD AND THEREFORE STILL A BOY.
I AM A MAN! I AM ALMOST EIGHTEEN YEARS OLD, AND I AM COMING WITH YOU!
MY SON, YOU STILL HAVE ANOTHER YEAR TO WAIT BEFORE YOU BEGIN YOUR TRAINING AS A SOLDIER.
BUT WHO WILL WATCH OVER YOU IN BATTLE IF I DO NOT COME?
YOUR REPUTATION PRECEDES YOU, EUSTACHIUS. THE IDEA OF YOU WATCHING MY BACK BRINGS MY BOY NO COMFORT AT ALL.
I HAVE YOUR FATHER'S BACK, CALLIAS. I PROMISE YOU THAT.
AND WHO HAS YOURS? IF WE WASTE ANY MORE TIME, CYRUS'S BATTLE WILL BE OVER. LET'S MOVE.

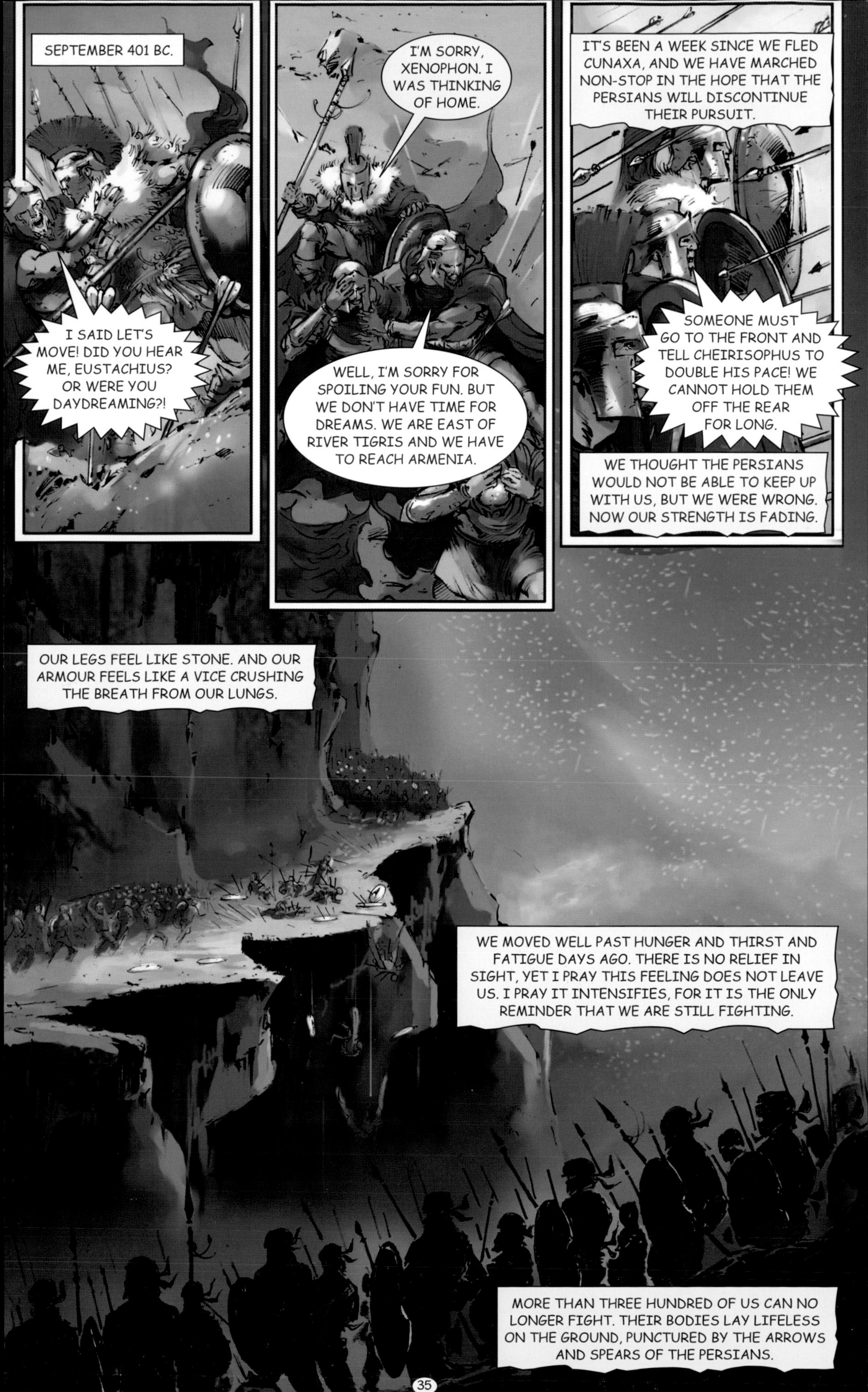
SEPTEMBER 401 BC.
I SAID LET'S MOVE! DID YOU HEAR ME, EUSTACHIUS? OR WERE YOU DAYDREAMING?!
I'M SORRY, XENOPHON. I WAS THINKING OF HOME.
WELL, I'M SORRY FOR SPOILING YOUR FUN. BUT WE DON'T HAVE TIME FOR DREAMS. WE ARE EAST OF RIVER TIGRIS AND WE HAVE TO REACH ARMENIA.
IT'S BEEN A WEEK SINCE WE FLED CUNAXA, AND WE HAVE MARCHED NON-STOP IN THE HOPE THAT THE PERSIANS WILL DISCONTINUE THEIR PURSUIT.
SOMEONE MUST GO TO THE FRONT AND TELL CHEIRISOPHUS TO DOUBLE HIS PACE! WE CANNOT HOLD THEM OFF THE REAR FOR LONG.
WE THOUGHT THE PERSIANS WOULD NOT BE ABLE TO KEEP UP WITH US, BUT WE WERE WRONG. NOW OUR STRENGTH IS FADING.
OUR LEGS FEEL LIKE STONE. AND OUR ARMOUR FEELS LIKE A VICE CRUSHING THE BREATH FROM OUR LUNGS.
WE MOVED WELL PAST HUNGER AND THIRST AND FATIGUE DAYS AGO. THERE IS NO RELIEF IN SIGHT, YET I PRAY THIS FEELING DOES NOT LEAVE US. I PRAY IT INTENSIFIES, FOR IT IS THE ONLY REMINDER THAT WE ARE STILL FIGHTING.
MORE THAN THREE HUNDRED OF US CAN NO LONGER FIGHT. THEIR BODIES LAY LIFELESS ON THE GROUND, PUNCTURED BY THE ARROWS AND SPEARS OF THE PERSIANS.

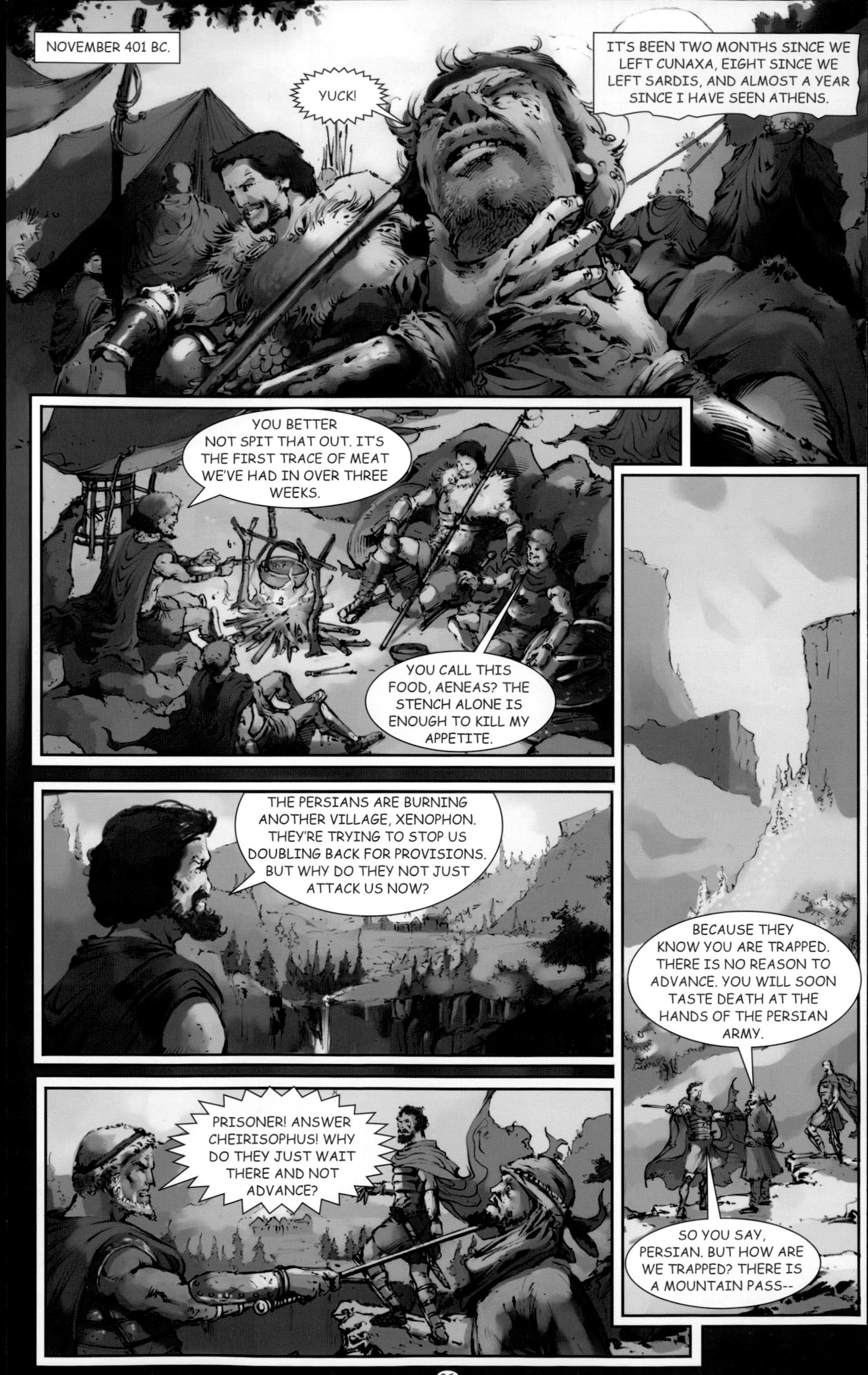
NOVEMBER 401 BC.
YUCK!
IT'S BEEN TWO MONTHS SINCE WE LEFT CUNAXA, EIGHT SINCE WE LEFT SARDIS, AND ALMOST A YEAR SINCE I HAVE SEEN ATHENS.
YOU BETTER NOT SPIT THAT OUT. IT'S THE FIRST TRACE OF MEAT WE'VE HAD IN OVER THREE WEEKS.
YOU CALL THIS FOOD, AENEAS? THE STENCH ALONE IS ENOUGH TO KILL MY APPETITE.
THE PERSIANS ARE BURNING ANOTHER VILLAGE, XENOPHON. THEY'RE TRYING TO STOP US DOUBLING BACK FOR PROVISIONS. BUT WHY DO THEY NOT JUST ATTACK US NOW?
PRISONER! ANSWER CHEIRISOPHUS! WHY DO THEY JUST WAIT THERE AND NOT ADVANCE?
BECAUSE THEY KNOW YOU ARE TRAPPED. THERE IS NO REASON TO ADVANCE. YOU WILL SOON TASTE DEATH AT THE HANDS OF THE PERSIAN ARMY.
SO YOU SAY, PERSIAN. BUT HOW ARE WE TRAPPED? THERE IS A MOUNTAIN PASS--

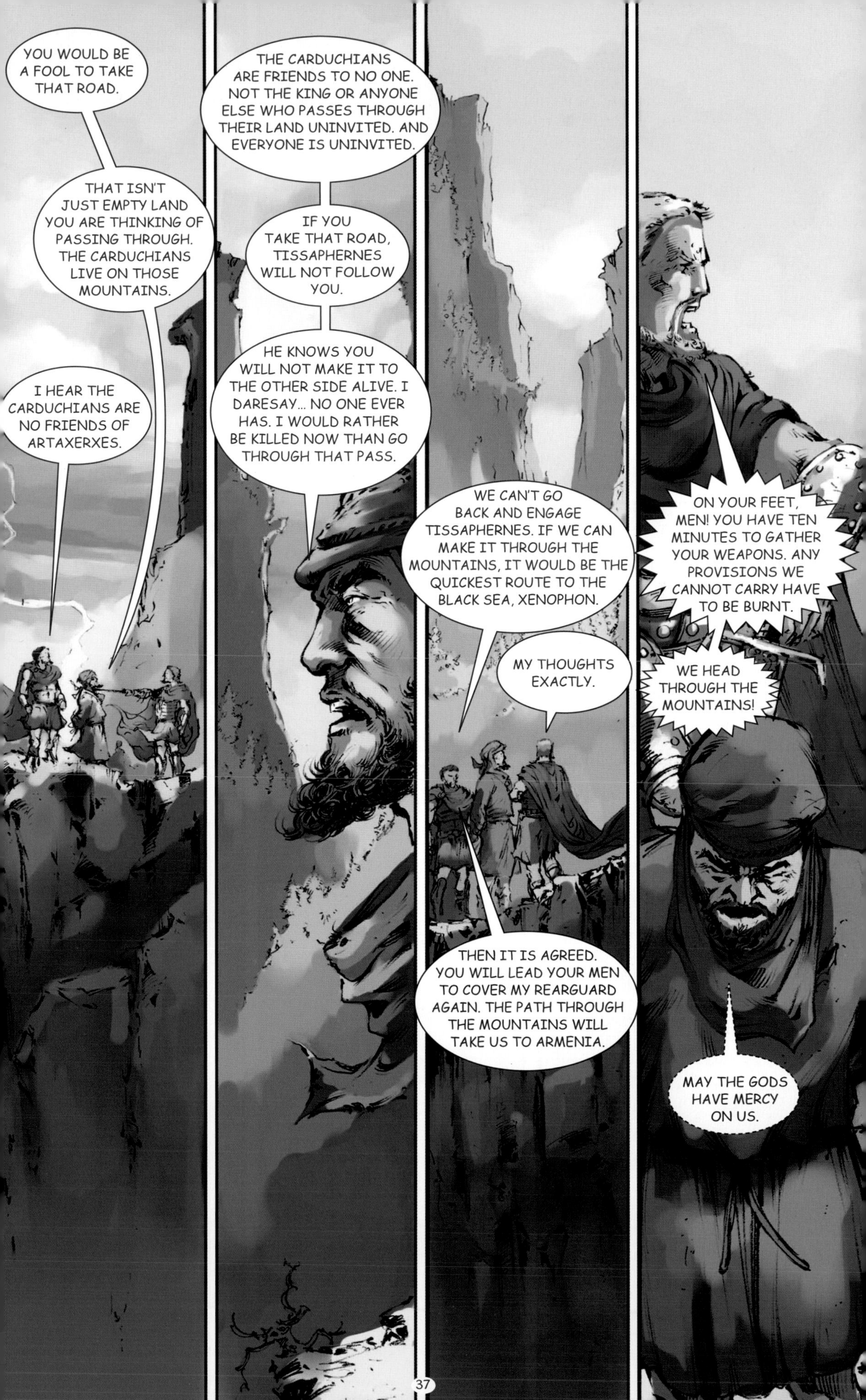
YOU WOULD BE A FOOL TO TAKE THAT ROAD.
THAT ISN'T JUST EMPTY LAND YOU ARE THINKING OF PASSING THROUGH. THE CARDUCHIANS LIVE ON THOSE MOUNTAINS.
I HEAR THE CARDUCHIANS ARE NO FRIENDS OF ARTAXERXES.
THE CARDUCHIANS ARE FRIENDS TO NO ONE. NOT THE KING OR ANYONE ELSE WHO PASSES THROUGH THEIR LAND UNINVITED. AND EVERYONE IS UNINVITED.
IF YOU TAKE THAT ROAD, TISSAPHERNES WILL NOT FOLLOW YOU.
HE KNOWS YOU WILL NOT MAKE IT TO THE OTHER SIDE ALIVE. I DARESAY... NO ONE EVER HAS. I WOULD RATHER BE KILLED NOW THAN GO THROUGH THAT PASS.
WE CAN'T GO BACK AND ENGAGE TISSAPHERNES. IF WE CAN MAKE IT THROUGH THE MOUNTAINS, IT WOULD BE THE QUICKEST ROUTE TO THE BLACK SEA, XENOPHON.
MY THOUGHTS EXACTLY.
THEN IT IS AGREED. YOU WILL LEAD YOUR MEN TO COVER MY REARGUARD AGAIN. THE PATH THROUGH THE MOUNTAINS WILL TAKE US TO ARMENIA.
ON YOUR FEET, MEN! YOU HAVE TEN MINUTES TO GATHER YOUR WEAPONS. ANY PROVISIONS WE CANNOT CARRY HAVE TO BE BURNT.
WE HEAD THROUGH THE MOUNTAINS!
MAY THE GODS HAVE MERCY ON US.

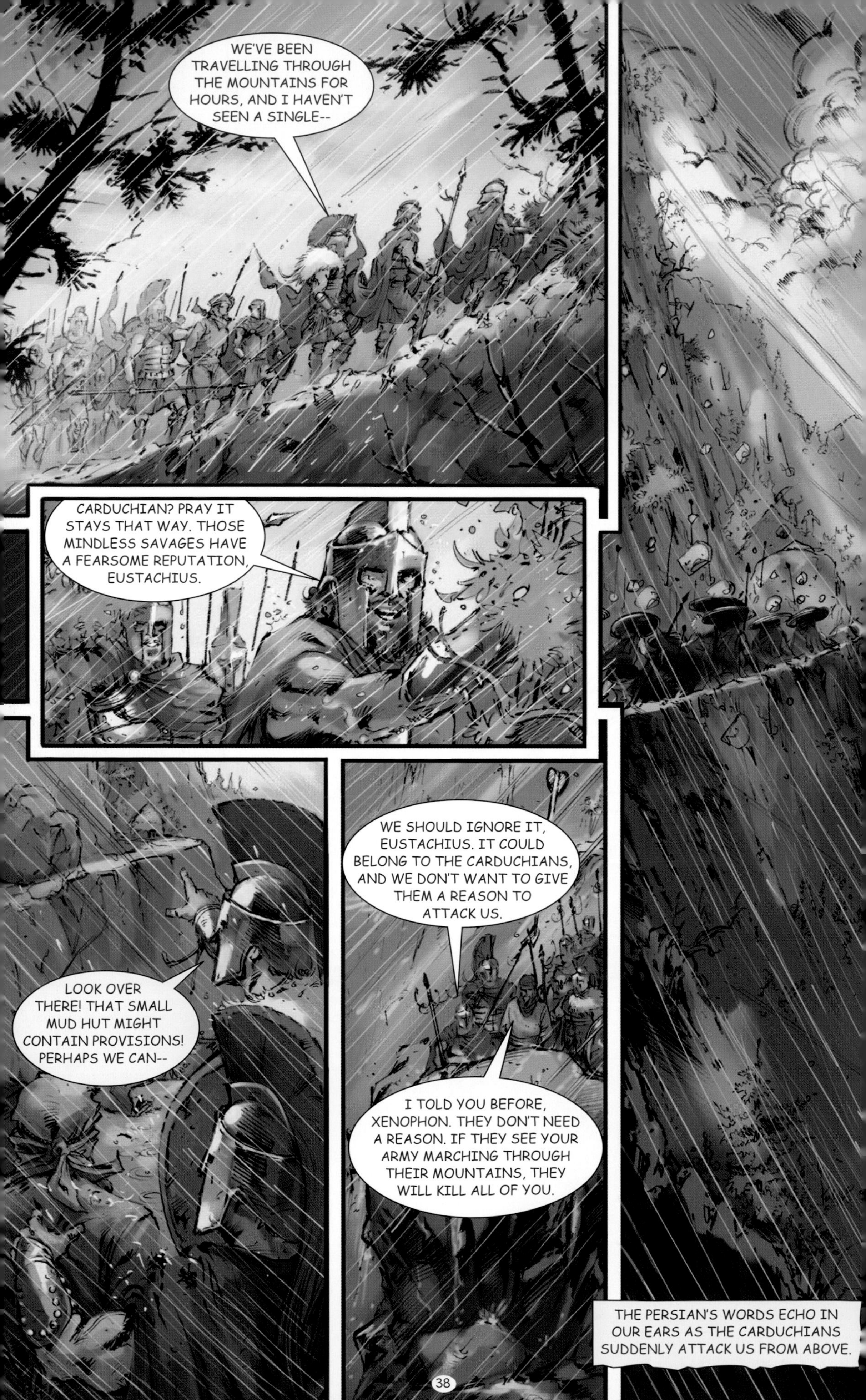
WE'VE BEEN TRAVELLING THROUGH THE MOUNTAINS FOR HOURS, AND I HAVEN'T SEEN A SINGLE--
CARDUCHIAN? PRAY IT STAYS THAT WAY. THOSE MINDLESS SAVAGES HAVE A FEARSOME REPUTATION, EUSTACHIUS.
LOOK OVER THERE! THAT SMALL MUD HUT MIGHT CONTAIN PROVISIONS! PERHAPS WE CAN--
WE SHOULD IGNORE IT, EUSTACHIUS. IT COULD BELONG TO THE CARDUCHIANS, AND WE DON'T WANT TO GIVE THEM A REASON TO ATTACK US.
I TOLD YOU BEFORE, XENOPHON. THEY DON'T NEED A REASON. IF THEY SEE YOUR ARMY MARCHING THROUGH THEIR MOUNTAINS, THEY WILL KILL ALL OF YOU.
THE PERSIAN'S WORDS ECHO IN OUR EARS AS THE CARDUCHIANS SUDDENLY ATTACK US FROM ABOVE.

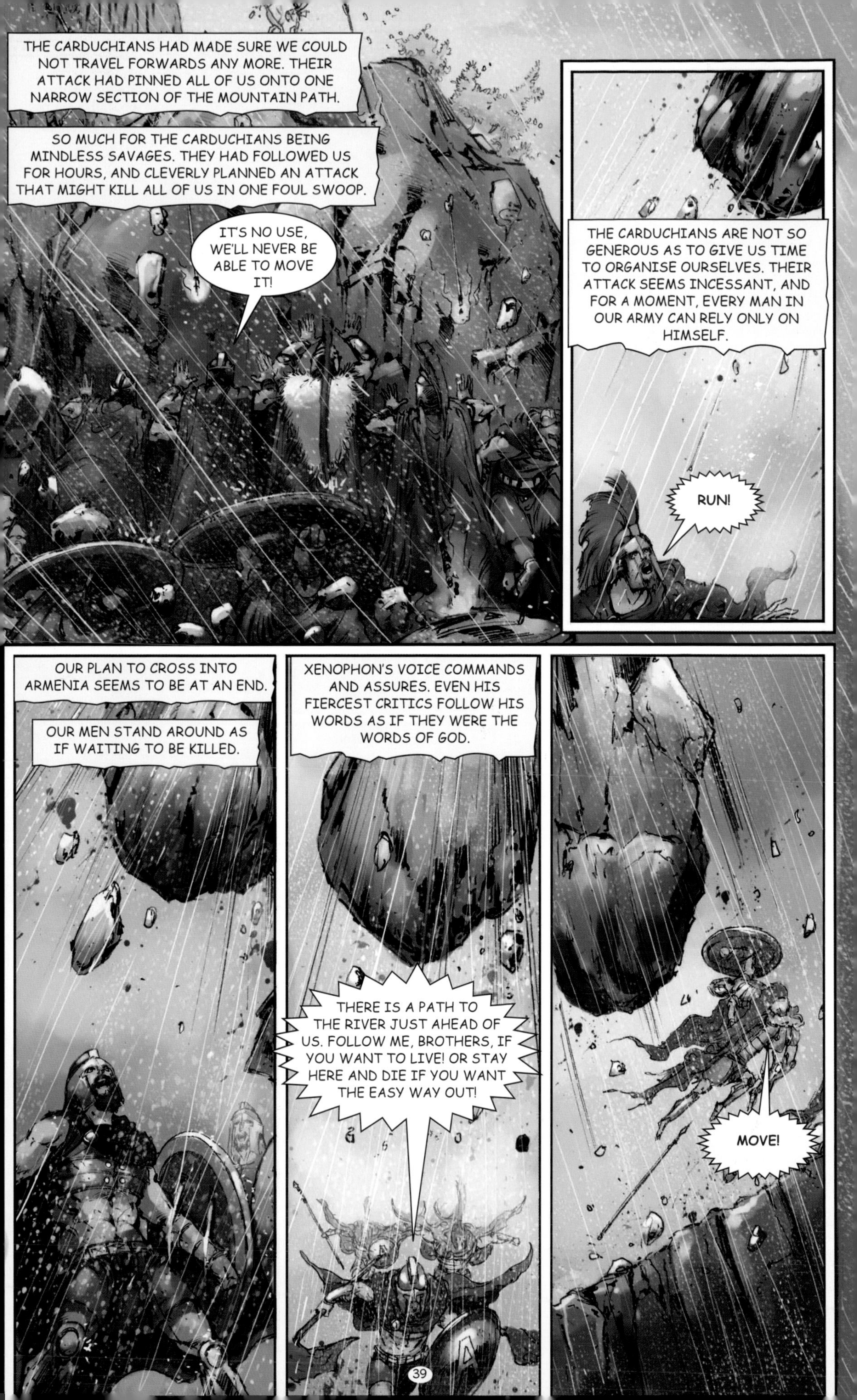
THE CARDUCHIANS HAD MADE SURE WE COULD NOT TRAVEL FORWARDS ANY MORE. THEIR ATTACK HAD PINNED ALL OF US ONTO ONE NARROW SECTION OF THE MOUNTAIN PATH.
SO MUCH FOR THE CARDUCHIANS BEING MINDLESS SAVAGES. THEY HAD FOLLOWED US FOR HOURS, AND CLEVERLY PLANNED AN ATTACK THAT MIGHT KILL ALL OF US IN ONE FOUL SWOOP.
IT'S NO USE, WE'LL NEVER BE ABLE TO MOVE IT!
THE CARDUCHIANS ARE NOT SO GENEROUS AS TO GIVE US TIME TO ORGANISE OURSELVES. THEIR ATTACK SEEMS INCESSANT, AND FOR A MOMENT, EVERY MAN IN OUR ARMY CAN RELY ONLY ON HIMSELF.
RUN!
OUR PLAN TO CROSS INTO ARMENIA SEEMS TO BE AT AN END.
OUR MEN STAND AROUND AS IF WAITING TO BE KILLED.
XENOPHON'S VOICE COMMANDS AND ASSURES. EVEN HIS FIERCEST CRITICS FOLLOW HIS WORDS AS IF THEY WERE THE WORDS OF GOD.
THERE IS A PATH TO THE RIVER JUST AHEAD OF US. FOLLOW ME, BROTHERS, IF YOU WANT TO LIVE! OR STAY HERE AND DIE IF YOU WANT THE EASY WAY OUT!
MOVE!

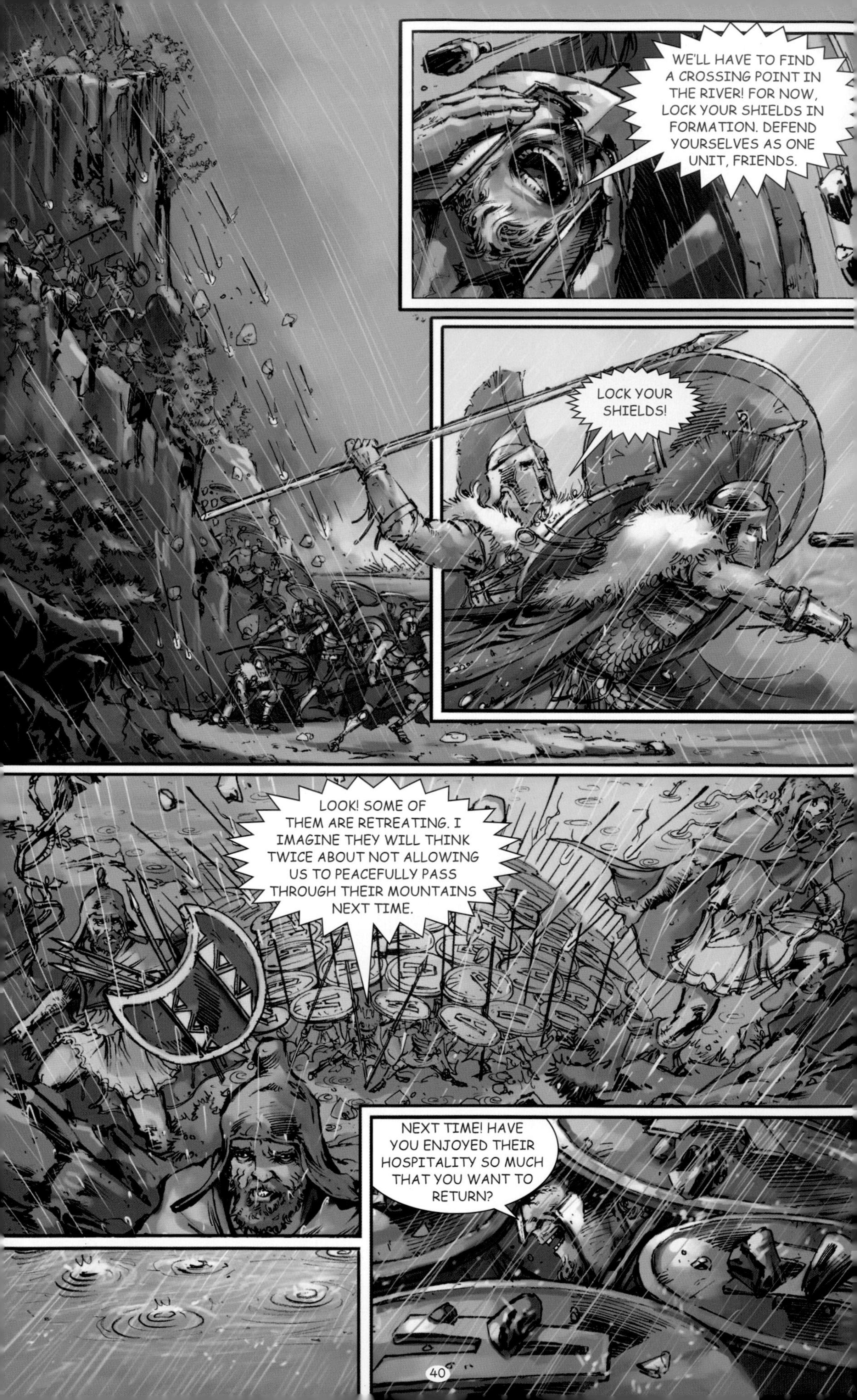
WE'LL HAVE TO FIND A CROSSING POINT IN THE RIVER! FOR NOW, LOCK YOUR SHIELDS IN FORMATION. DEFEND YOURSELVES AS ONE UNIT, FRIENDS.
LOCK YOUR SHIELDS!
LOOK! SOME OF THEM ARE RETREATING. I IMAGINE THEY WILL THINK TWICE ABOUT NOT ALLOWING US TO PEACEFULLY PASS THROUGH THEIR MOUNTAINS NEXT TIME.
NEXT TIME! HAVE YOU ENJOYED THEIR HOSPITALITY SO MUCH THAT YOU WANT TO RETURN?

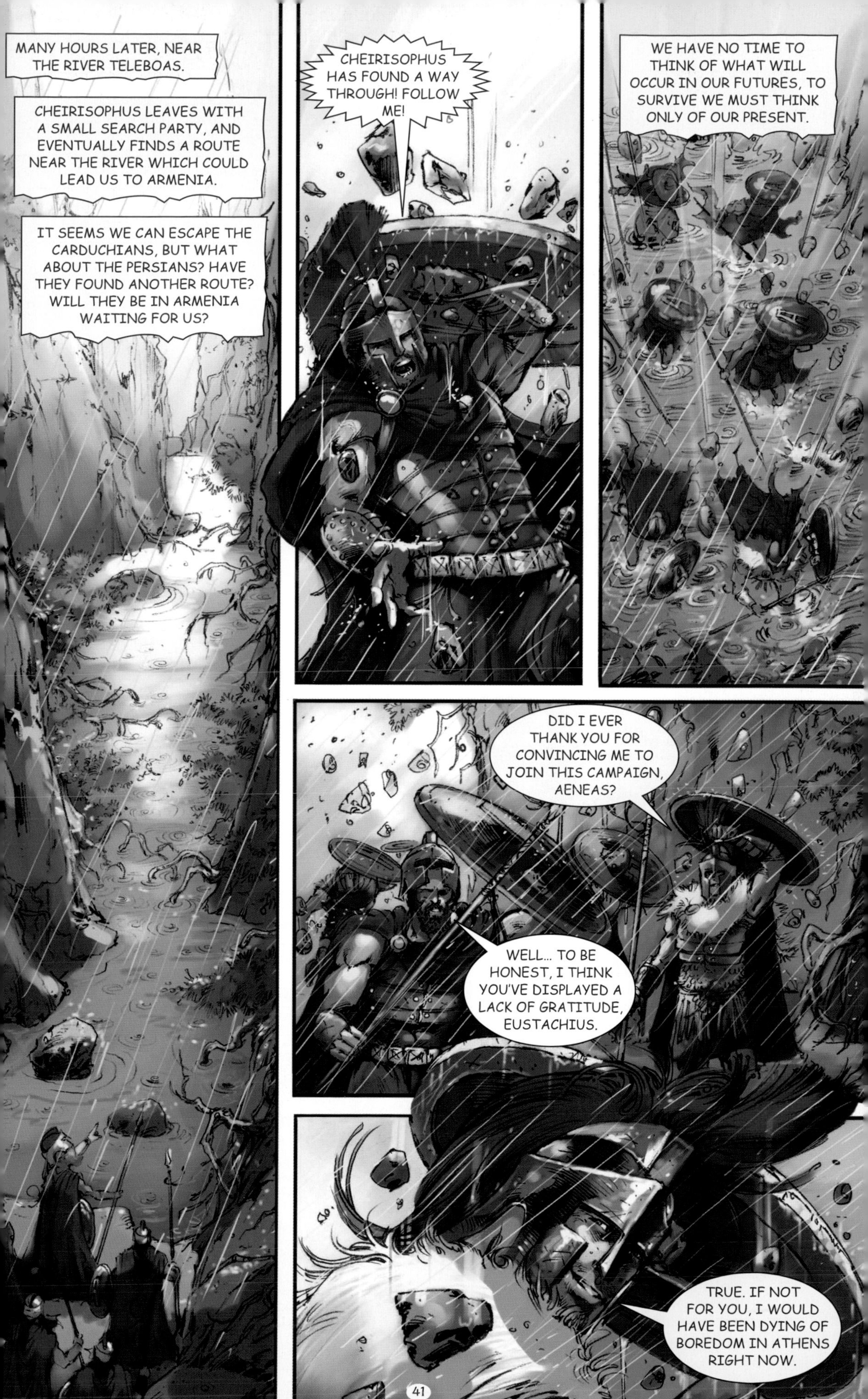
MANY HOURS LATER, NEAR THE RIVER TELEBOAS.
CHEIRISOPHUS LEAVES WITH A SMALL SEARCH PARTY, AND EVENTUALLY FINDS A ROUTE NEAR THE RIVER WHICH COULD LEAD US TO ARMENIA.
IT SEEMS WE CAN ESCAPE THE CARDUCHIANS, BUT WHAT ABOUT THE PERSIANS? HAVE THEY FOUND ANOTHER ROUTE? WILL THEY BE IN ARMENIA WAITING FOR US?
CHEIRISOPHUS HAS FOUND A WAY THROUGH! FOLLOW ME!
WE HAVE NO TIME TO THINK OF WHAT WILL OCCUR IN OUR FUTURES, TO SURVIVE WE MUST THINK ONLY OF OUR PRESENT.
DID I EVER THANK YOU FOR CONVINCING ME TO JOIN THIS CAMPAIGN, AENEAS?
WELL... TO BE HONEST, I THINK YOU'VE DISPLAYED A LACK OF GRATITUDE, EUSTACHIUS.
TRUE. IF NOT FOR YOU, I WOULD HAVE BEEN DYING OF BOREDOM IN ATHENS RIGHT NOW.

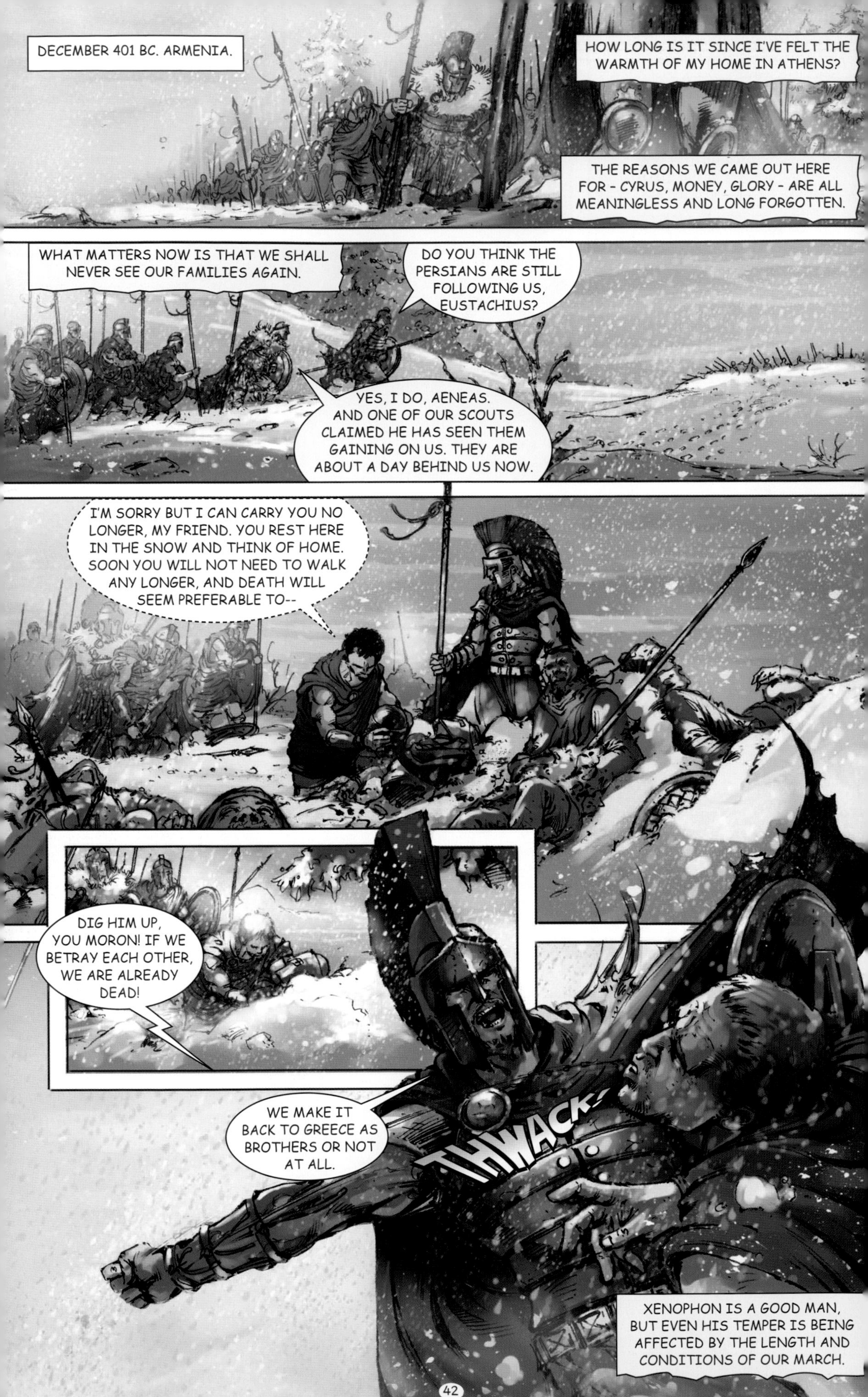
DECEMBER 401 BC. ARMENIA.
HOW LONG IS IT SINCE I'VE FELT THE WARMTH OF MY HOME IN ATHENS?
THE REASONS WE CAME OUT HERE FOR - CYRUS, MONEY, GLORY - ARE ALL MEANINGLESS AND LONG FORGOTTEN.
WHAT MATTERS NOW IS THAT WE SHALL NEVER SEE OUR FAMILIES AGAIN.
DO YOU THINK THE PERSIANS ARE STILL FOLLOWING US, EUSTACHIUS?
YES, I DO, AENEAS. AND ONE OF OUR SCOUTS CLAIMED HE HAS SEEN THEM GAINING ON US. THEY ARE ABOUT A DAY BEHIND US NOW.
I'M SORRY BUT I CAN CARRY YOU NO LONGER, MY FRIEND. YOU REST HERE IN THE SNOW AND THINK OF HOME. SOON YOU WILL NOT NEED TO WALK ANY LONGER, AND DEATH WILL SEEM PREFERABLE TO--
DIG HIM UP, YOU MORON! IF WE BETRAY EACH OTHER, WE ARE ALREADY DEAD!
THWACK!
WE MAKE IT BACK TO GREECE AS BROTHERS OR NOT AT ALL.
XENOPHON IS A GOOD MAN, BUT EVEN HIS TEMPER IS BEING AFFECTED BY THE LENGTH AND CONDITIONS OF OUR MARCH.

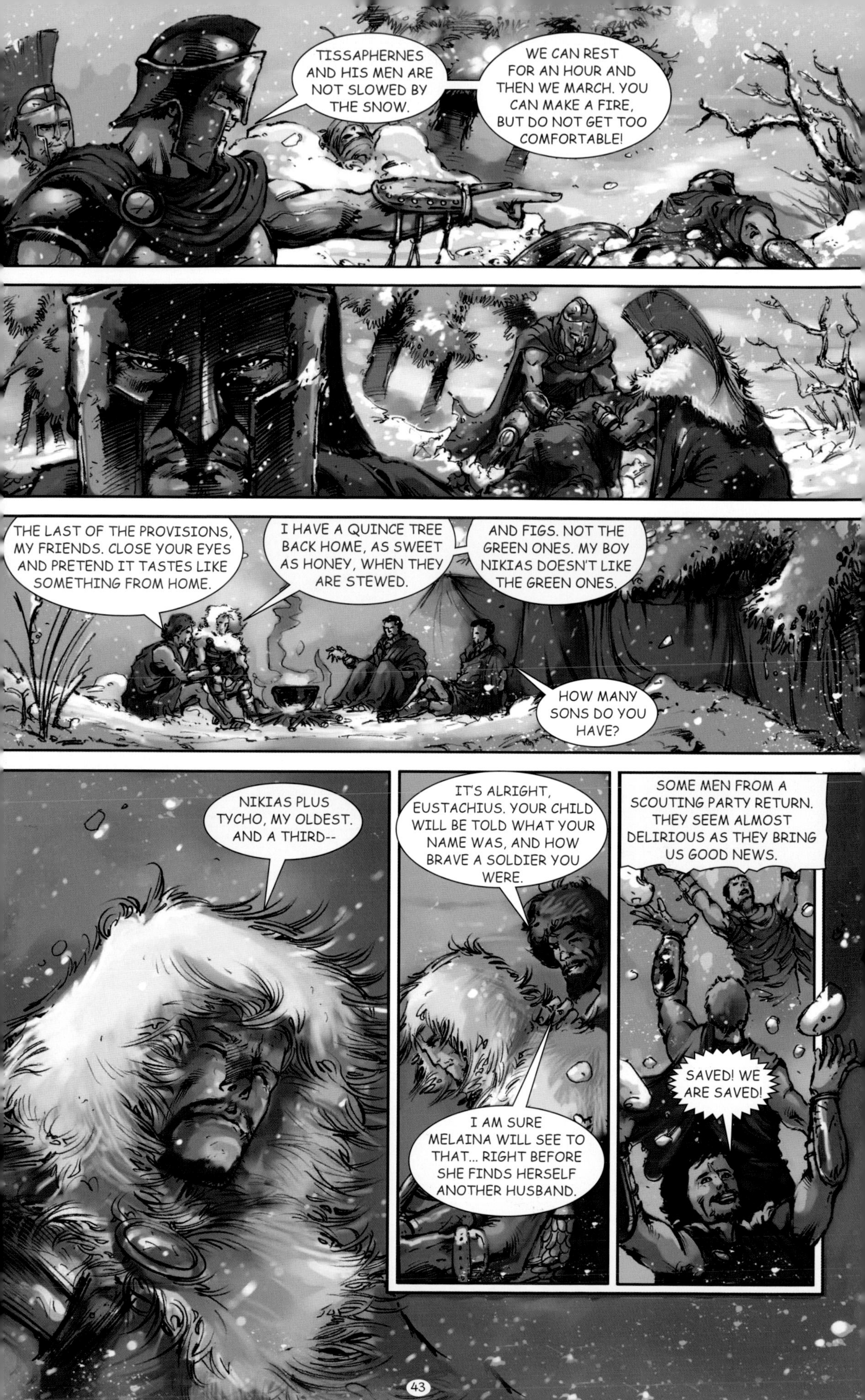
TISSAPHERNES AND HIS MEN ARE NOT SLOWED BY THE SNOW.
WE CAN REST FOR AN HOUR AND THEN WE MARCH. YOU CAN MAKE A FIRE, BUT DO NOT GET TOO COMFORTABLE!
THE LAST OF THE PROVISIONS, MY FRIENDS. CLOSE YOUR EYES AND PRETEND IT TASTES LIKE SOMETHING FROM HOME.
I HAVE A QUINCE TREE BACK HOME, AS SWEET AS HONEY, WHEN THEY ARE STEWED.
AND FIGS. NOT THE GREEN ONES. MY BOY NIKIAS DOESN'T LIKE THE GREEN ONES.
HOW MANY SONS DO YOU HAVE?
NIKIAS PLUS TYCHO, MY OLDEST. AND A THIRD--
IT'S ALRIGHT, EUSTACHIUS. YOUR CHILD WILL BE TOLD WHAT YOUR NAME WAS, AND HOW BRAVE A SOLDIER YOU WERE.
I AM SURE MELAINA WILL SEE TO THAT... RIGHT BEFORE SHE FINDS HERSELF ANOTHER HUSBAND.
SOME MEN FROM A SCOUTING PARTY RETURN. THEY SEEM ALMOST DELIRIOUS AS THEY BRING US GOOD NEWS.
SAVED! WE ARE SAVED!

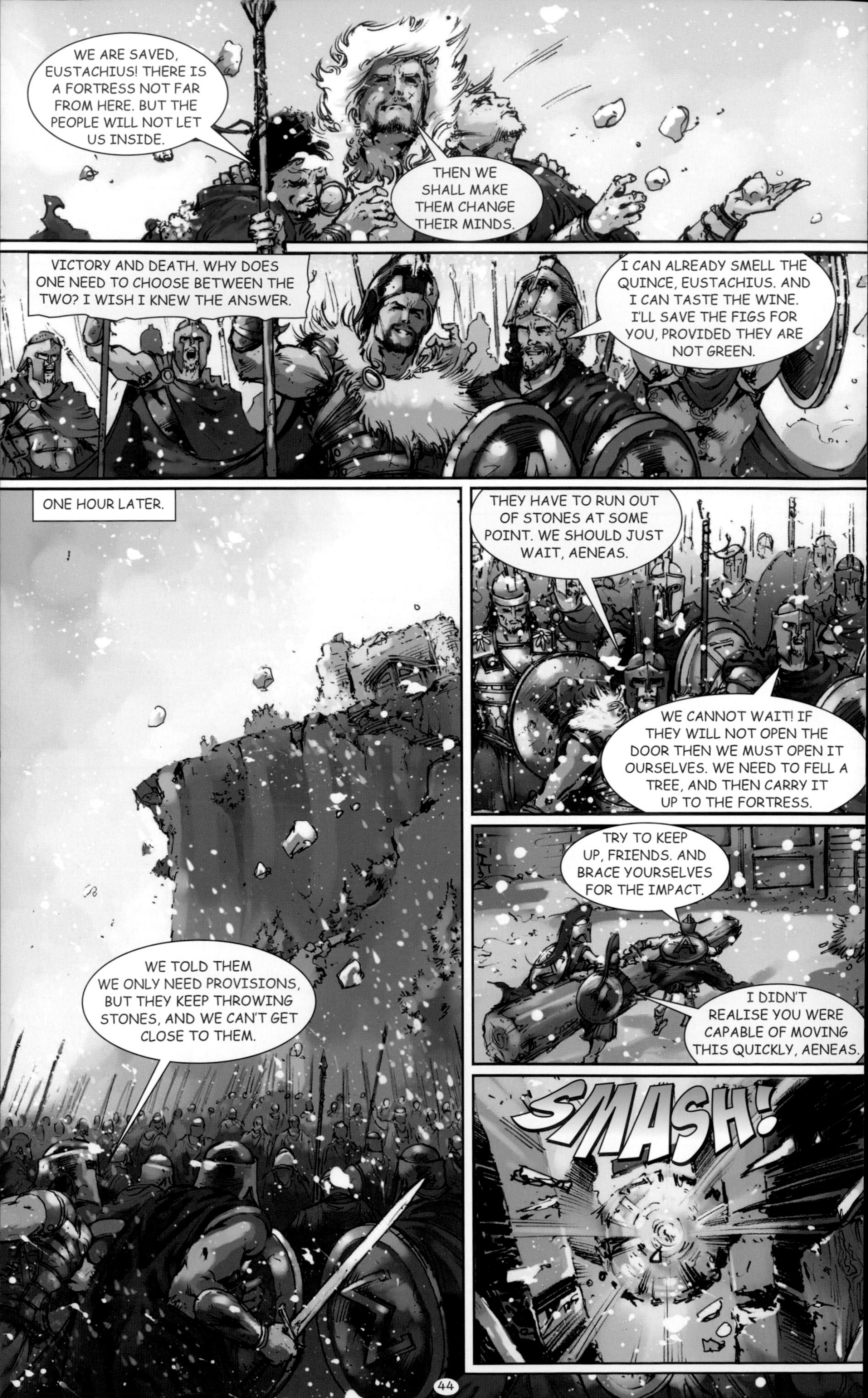
WE ARE SAVED, EUSTACHIUS! THERE IS A FORTRESS NOT FAR FROM HERE. BUT THE PEOPLE WILL NOT LET US INSIDE.
THEN WE SHALL MAKE THEM CHANGE THEIR MINDS.
VICTORY AND DEATH. WHY DOES ONE NEED TO CHOOSE BETWEEN THE TWO? I WISH I KNEW THE ANSWER.
I CAN ALREADY SMELL THE QUINCE, EUSTACHIUS. AND I CAN TASTE THE WINE. I'LL SAVE THE FIGS FOR YOU, PROVIDED THEY ARE NOT GREEN.
ONE HOUR LATER.
WE TOLD THEM WE ONLY NEED PROVISIONS, BUT THEY KEEP THROWING STONES, AND WE CAN'T GET CLOSE TO THEM.
THEY HAVE TO RUN OUT OF STONES AT SOME POINT. WE SHOULD JUST WAIT, AENEAS.
WE CANNOT WAIT! IF THEY WILL NOT OPEN THE DOOR THEN WE MUST OPEN IT OURSELVES. WE NEED TO FELL A TREE, AND THEN CARRY IT UP TO THE FORTRESS.
TRY TO KEEP UP, FRIENDS. AND BRACE YOURSELVES FOR THE IMPACT.
I DIDN'T REALISE YOU WERE CAPABLE OF MOVING THIS QUICKLY, AENEAS.
SMASH!

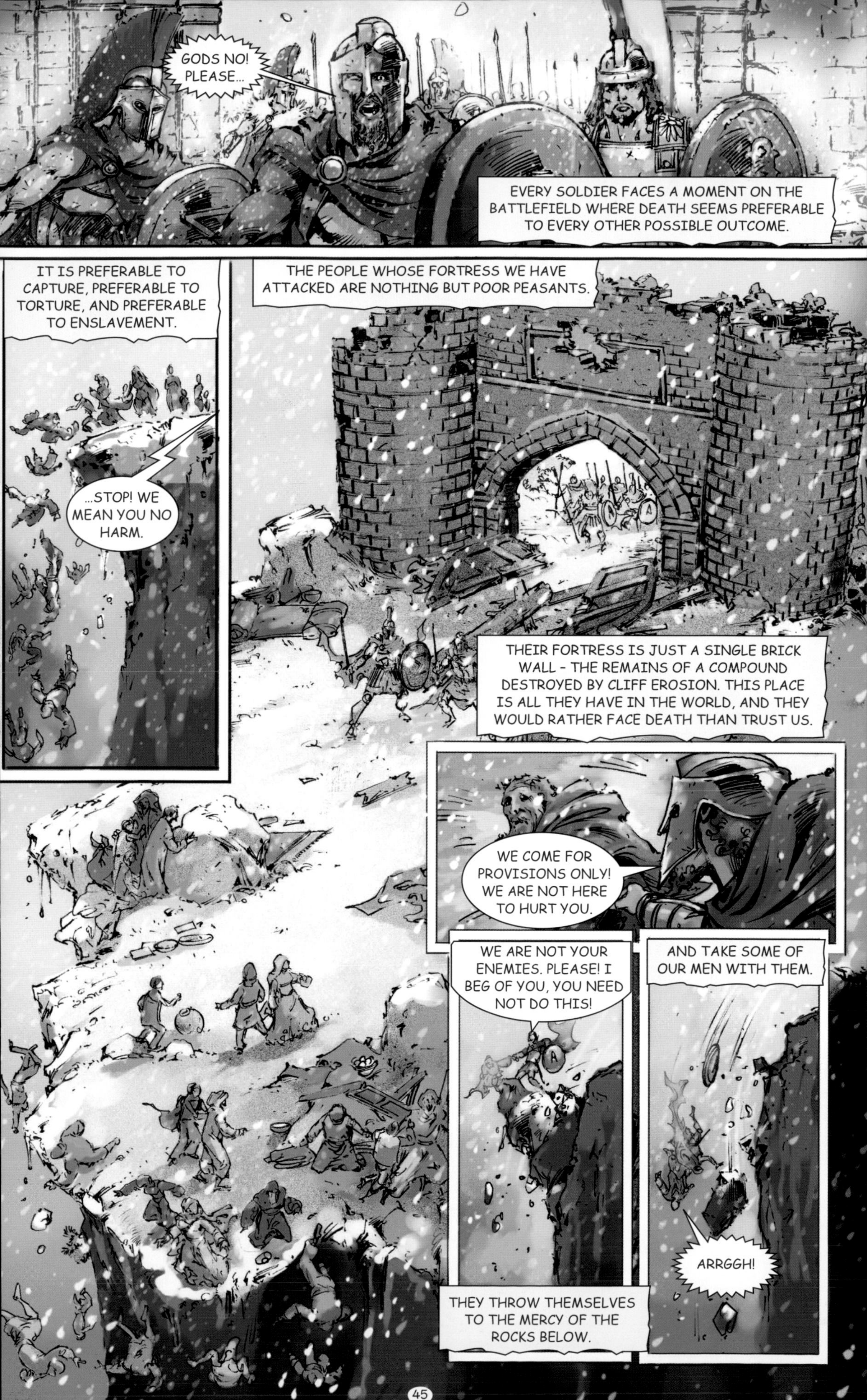
GODS NO! PLEASE...
EVERY SOLDIER FACES A MOMENT ON THE BATTLEFIELD WHERE DEATH SEEMS PREFERABLE TO EVERY OTHER POSSIBLE OUTCOME.
IT IS PREFERABLE TO CAPTURE, PREFERABLE TO TORTURE, AND PREFERABLE TO ENSLAVEMENT.
THE PEOPLE WHOSE FORTRESS WE HAVE ATTACKED ARE NOTHING BUT POOR PEASANTS.
...STOP! WE MEAN YOU NO HARM.
THEIR FORTRESS IS JUST A SINGLE BRICK WALL - THE REMAINS OF A COMPOUND DESTROYED BY CLIFF EROSION. THIS PLACE IS ALL THEY HAVE IN THE WORLD, AND THEY WOULD RATHER FACE DEATH THAN TRUST US.
WE COME FOR PROVISIONS ONLY! WE ARE NOT HERE TO HURT YOU.
WE ARE NOT YOUR ENEMIES. PLEASE! I BEG OF YOU, YOU NEED NOT DO THIS!
AND TAKE SOME OF OUR MEN WITH THEM.
ARRGGH!
THEY THROW THEMSELVES TO THE MERCY OF THE ROCKS BELOW.

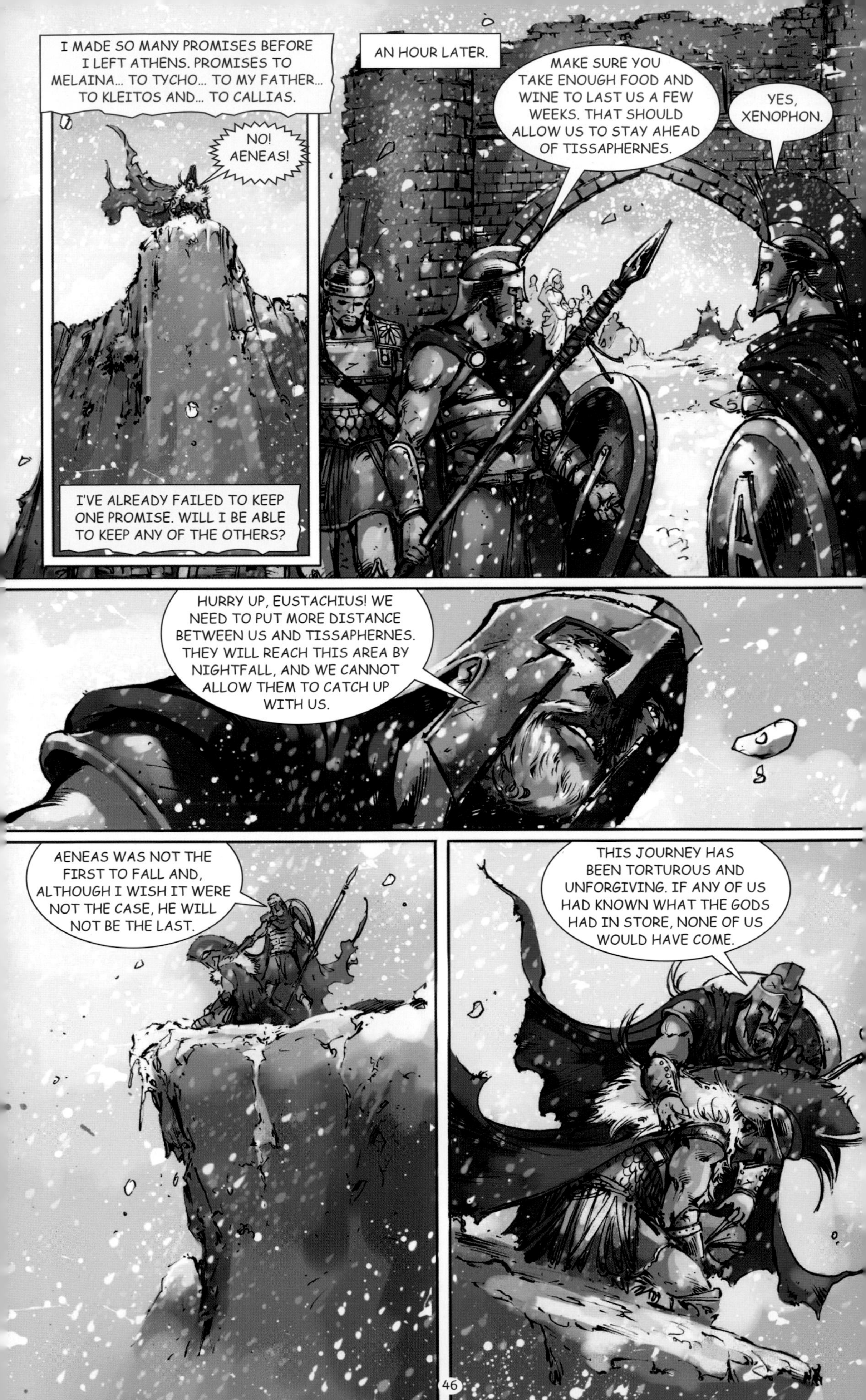
I MADE SO MANY PROMISES BEFORE I LEFT ATHENS. PROMISES TO MELAINA... TO TYCHO... TO MY FATHER... TO KLEITOS AND... TO CALLIAS.
NO! AENEAS!
I'VE ALREADY FAILED TO KEEP ONE PROMISE. WILL I BE ABLE TO KEEP ANY OF THE OTHERS?
AN HOUR LATER.
MAKE SURE YOU TAKE ENOUGH FOOD AND WINE TO LAST US A FEW WEEKS. THAT SHOULD ALLOW US TO STAY AHEAD OF TISSAPHERNES.
YES, XENOPHON.
HURRY UP, EUSTACHIUS! WE NEED TO PUT MORE DISTANCE BETWEEN US AND TISSAPHERNES. THEY WILL REACH THIS AREA BY NIGHTFALL, AND WE CANNOT ALLOW THEM TO CATCH UP WITH US.
AENEAS WAS NOT THE FIRST TO FALL AND, ALTHOUGH I WISH IT WERE NOT THE CASE, HE WILL NOT BE THE LAST.
THIS JOURNEY HAS BEEN TORTUROUS AND UNFORGIVING. IF ANY OF US HAD KNOWN WHAT THE GODS HAD IN STORE, NONE OF US WOULD HAVE COME.

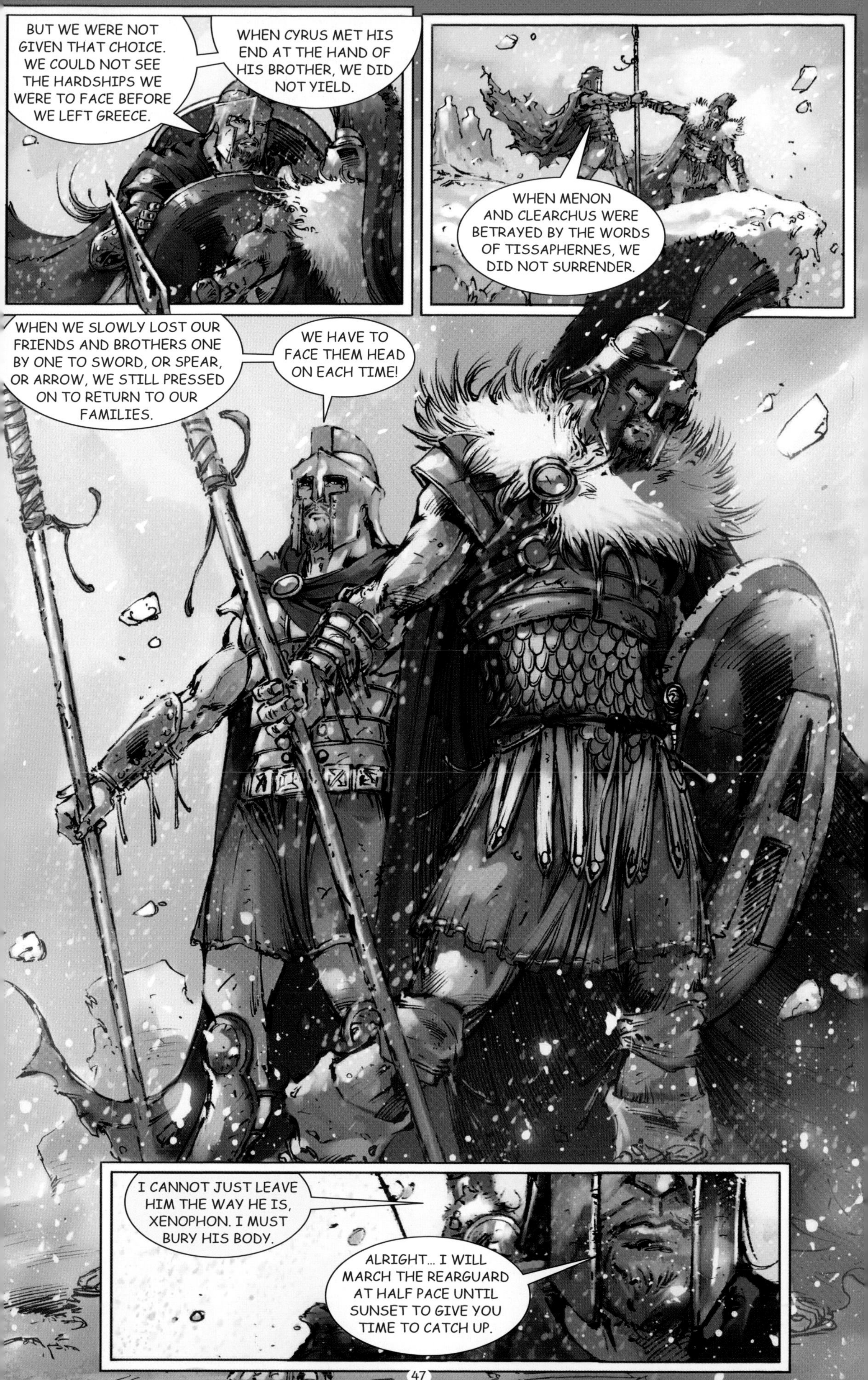
BUT WE WERE NOT GIVEN THAT CHOICE. WE COULD NOT SEE THE HARDSHIPS WE WERE TO FACE BEFORE WE LEFT GREECE.
WHEN CYRUS MET HIS END AT THE HAND OF HIS BROTHER, WE DID NOT YIELD.
WHEN MENON AND CLEARCHUS WERE BETRAYED BY THE WORDS OF TISSAPHERNES, WE DID NOT SURRENDER.
WHEN WE SLOWLY LOST OUR FRIENDS AND BROTHERS ONE BY ONE TO SWORD, OR SPEAR, OR ARROW, WE STILL PRESSED ON TO RETURN TO OUR FAMILIES.
WE HAVE TO FACE THEM HEAD ON EACH TIME!
I CANNOT JUST LEAVE HIM THE WAY HE IS, XENOPHON. I MUST BURY HIS BODY.
ALRIGHT... I WILL MARCH THE REARGUARD AT HALF PACE UNTIL SUNSET TO GIVE YOU TIME TO CATCH UP.

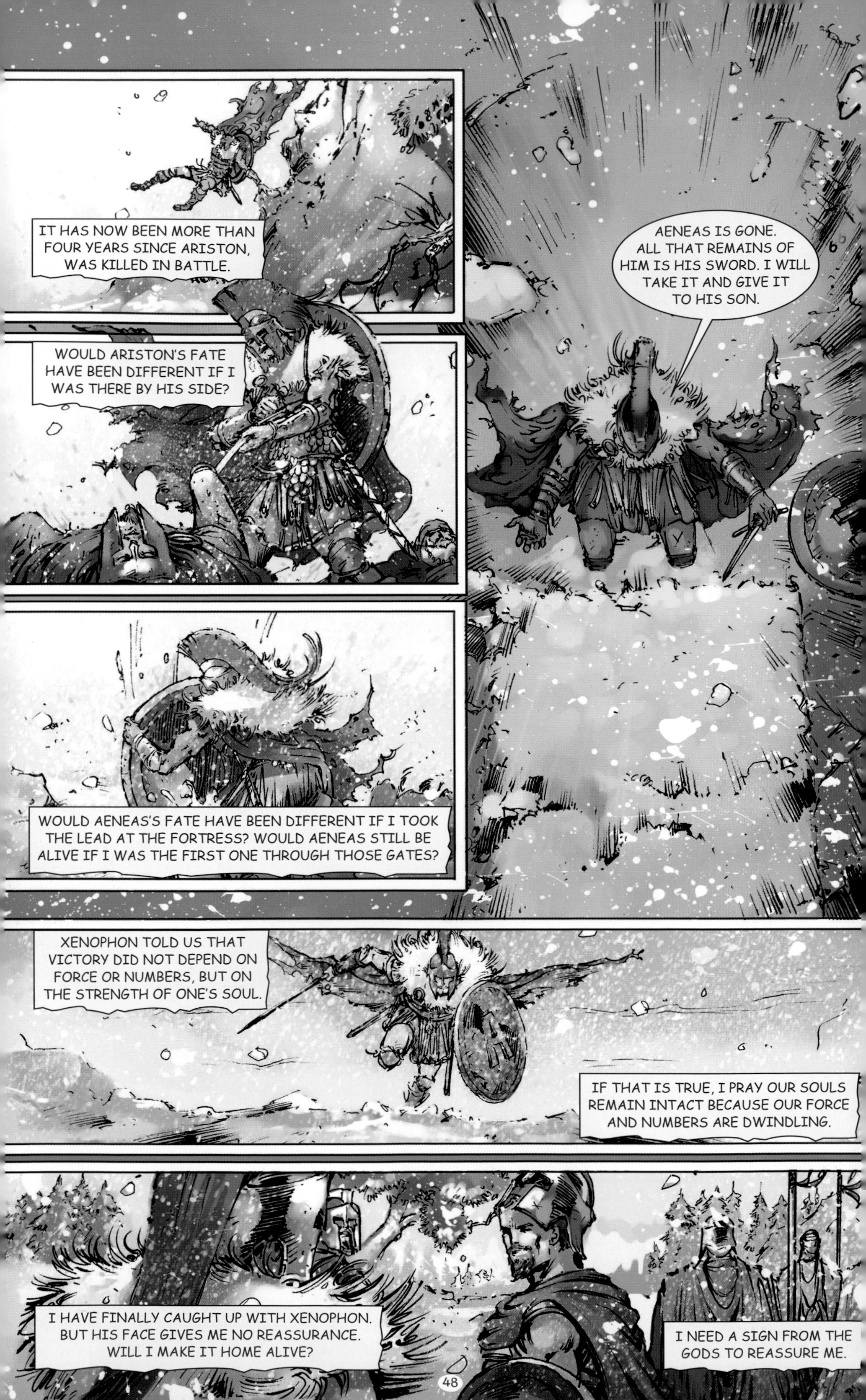
IT HAS NOW BEEN MORE THAN FOUR YEARS SINCE ARISTON, WAS KILLED IN BATTLE.
WOULD ARISTON'S FATE HAVE BEEN DIFFERENT IF I WAS THERE BY HIS SIDE?
WOULD AENEAS'S FATE HAVE BEEN DIFFERENT IF I TOOK THE LEAD AT THE FORTRESS? WOULD AENEAS STILL BE ALIVE IF I WAS THE FIRST ONE THROUGH THOSE GATES?
AENEAS IS GONE. ALL THAT REMAINS OF HIM IS HIS SWORD. I WILL TAKE IT AND GIVE IT TO HIS SON.
XENOPHON TOLD US THAT VICTORY DID NOT DEPEND ON FORCE OR NUMBERS, BUT ON THE STRENGTH OF ONE'S SOUL.
IF THAT IS TRUE, I PRAY OUR SOULS REMAIN INTACT BECAUSE OUR FORCE AND NUMBERS ARE DWINDLING.
I HAVE FINALLY CAUGHT UP WITH XENOPHON. BUT HIS FACE GIVES ME NO REASSURANCE. WILL I MAKE IT HOME ALIVE?
I NEED A SIGN FROM THE GODS TO REASSURE ME.

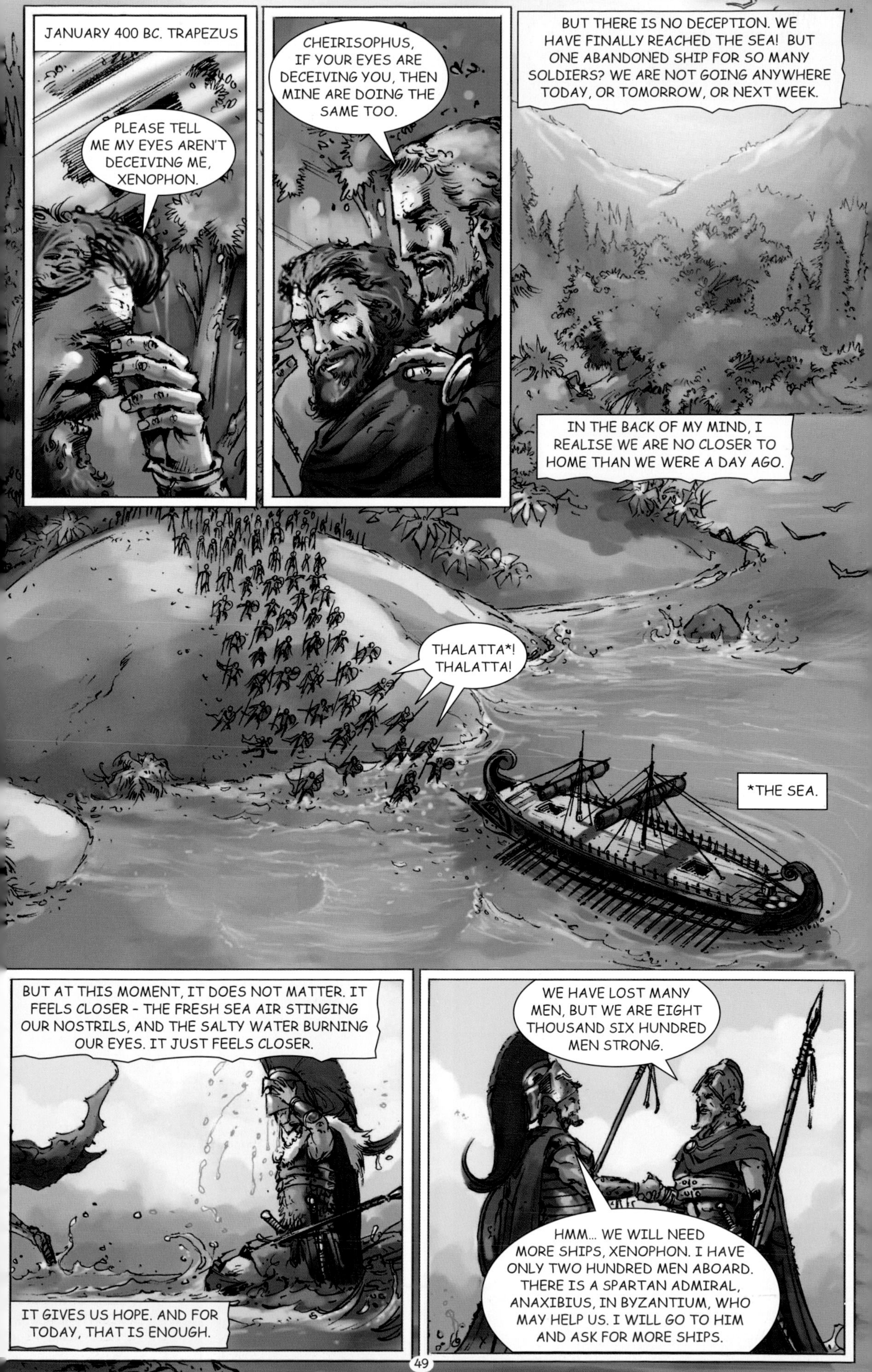
JANUARY 400 BC. TRAPEZUS
PLEASE TELL ME MY EYES AREN'T DECEIVING ME, XENOPHON.
CHEIRISOPHUS, IF YOUR EYES ARE DECEIVING YOU, THEN MINE ARE DOING THE SAME TOO.
BUT THERE IS NO DECEPTION. WE HAVE FINALLY REACHED THE SEA! BUT ONE ABANDONED SHIP FOR SO MANY SOLDIERS? WE ARE NOT GOING ANYWHERE TODAY, OR TOMORROW, OR NEXT WEEK.
IN THE BACK OF MY MIND, I REALISE WE ARE NO CLOSER TO HOME THAN WE WERE A DAY AGO.
THALATTA*! THALATTA!
*THE SEA.
BUT AT THIS MOMENT, IT DOES NOT MATTER. IT FEELS CLOSER - THE FRESH SEA AIR STINGING OUR NOSTRILS, AND THE SALTY WATER BURNING OUR EYES. IT JUST FEELS CLOSER.
IT GIVES US HOPE. AND FOR TODAY, THAT IS ENOUGH.
WE HAVE LOST MANY MEN, BUT WE ARE EIGHT THOUSAND SIX HUNDRED MEN STRONG.
HMM... WE WILL NEED MORE SHIPS, XENOPHON. I HAVE ONLY TWO HUNDRED MEN ABOARD. THERE IS A SPARTAN ADMIRAL, ANAXIBIUS, IN BYZANTIUM, WHO MAY HELP US. I WILL GO TO HIM AND ASK FOR MORE SHIPS.

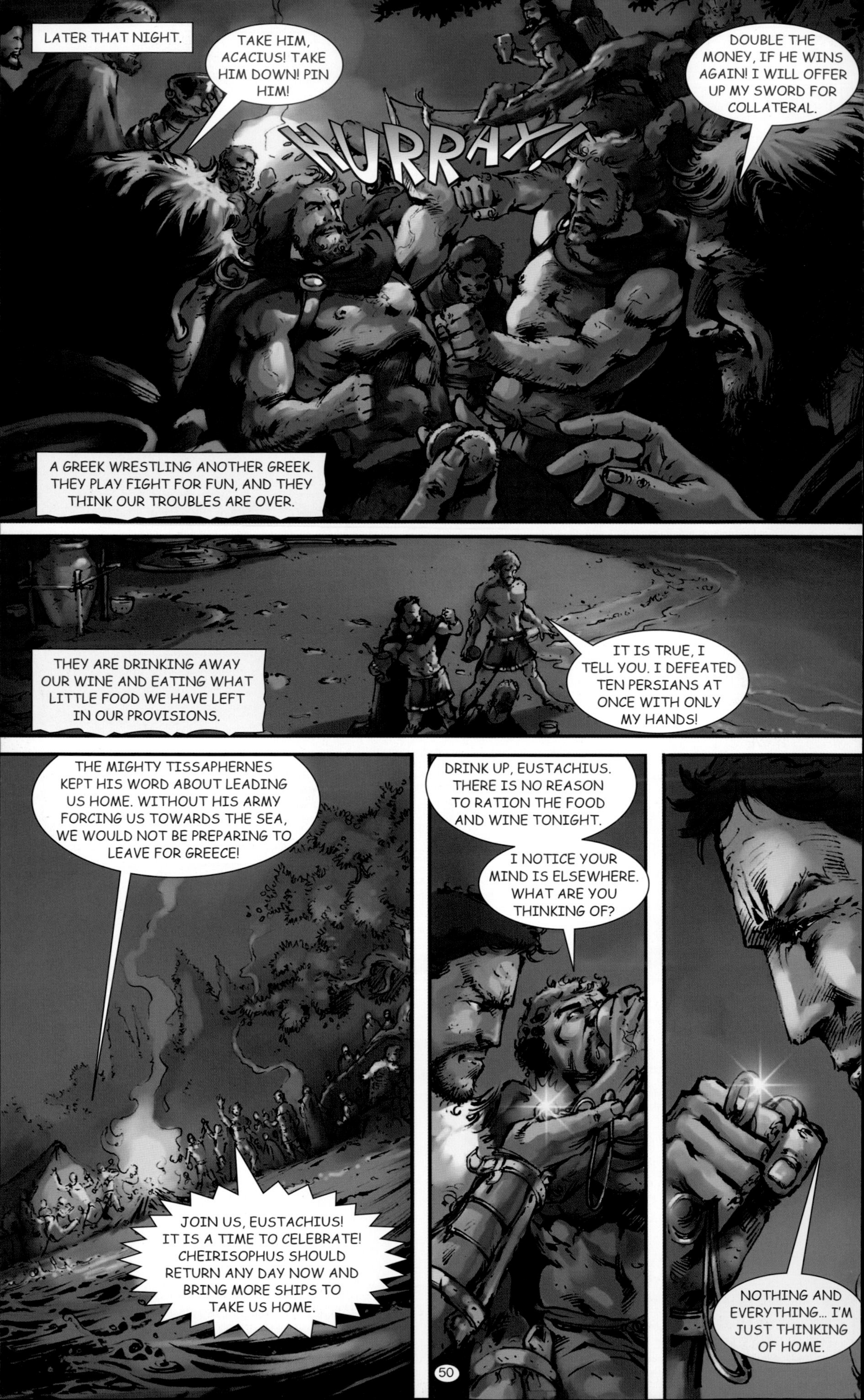
LATER THAT NIGHT.
TAKE HIM, ACACIUS! TAKE HIM DOWN! PIN HIM!
HURRAY!
DOUBLE THE MONEY, IF HE WINS AGAIN! I WILL OFFER UP MY SWORD FOR COLLATERAL.
A GREEK WRESTLING ANOTHER GREEK. THEY PLAY FIGHT FOR FUN, AND THEY THINK OUR TROUBLES ARE OVER.
THEY ARE DRINKING AWAY OUR WINE AND EATING WHAT LITTLE FOOD WE HAVE LEFT IN OUR PROVISIONS.
IT IS TRUE, I TELL YOU. I DEFEATED TEN PERSIANS AT ONCE WITH ONLY MY HANDS!
THE MIGHTY TISSAPHERNES KEPT HIS WORD ABOUT LEADING US HOME. WITHOUT HIS ARMY FORCING US TOWARDS THE SEA, WE WOULD NOT BE PREPARING TO LEAVE FOR GREECE!
JOIN US, EUSTACHIUS! IT IS A TIME TO CELEBRATE! CHEIRISOPHUS SHOULD RETURN ANY DAY NOW AND BRING MORE SHIPS TO TAKE US HOME.
DRINK UP, EUSTACHIUS. THERE IS NO REASON TO RATION THE FOOD AND WINE TONIGHT.
I NOTICE YOUR MIND IS ELSEWHERE. WHAT ARE YOU THINKING OF?
NOTHING AND EVERYTHING... I'M JUST THINKING OF HOME.

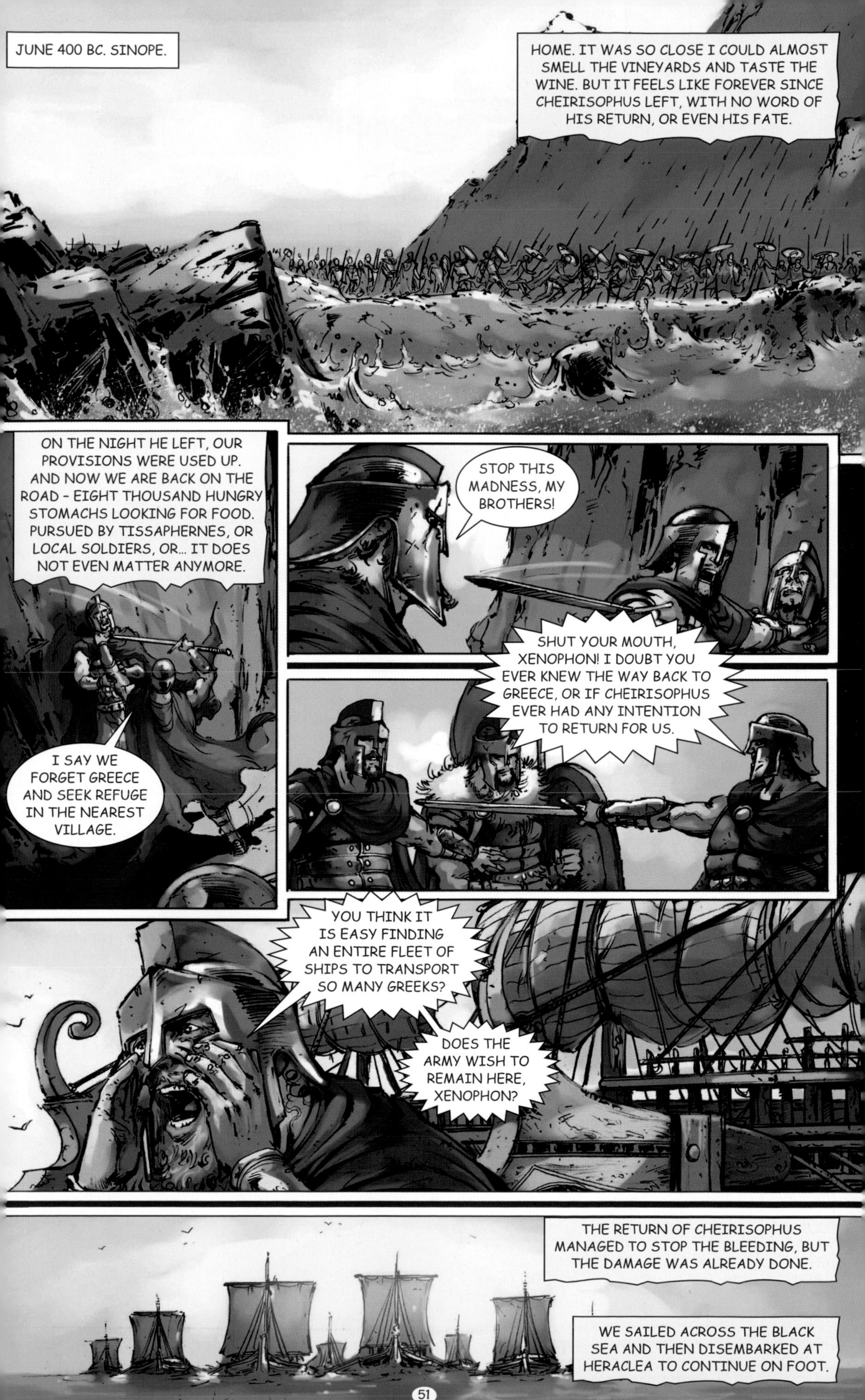
JUNE 400 BC. SINOPE.
HOME. IT WAS SO CLOSE I COULD ALMOST SMELL THE VINEYARDS AND TASTE THE WINE. BUT IT FEELS LIKE FOREVER SINCE CHEIRISOPHUS LEFT, WITH NO WORD OF HIS RETURN, OR EVEN HIS FATE.
ON THE NIGHT HE LEFT, OUR PROVISIONS WERE USED UP. AND NOW WE ARE BACK ON THE ROAD – EIGHT THOUSAND HUNGRY STOMACHS LOOKING FOR FOOD. PURSUED BY TISSAPHERNES, OR LOCAL SOLDIERS, OR... IT DOES NOT EVEN MATTER ANYMORE.
I SAY WE FORGET GREECE AND SEEK REFUGE IN THE NEAREST VILLAGE.
STOP THIS MADNESS, MY BROTHERS!
SHUT YOUR MOUTH, XENOPHON! I DOUBT YOU EVER KNEW THE WAY BACK TO GREECE, OR IF CHEIRISOPHUS EVER HAD ANY INTENTION TO RETURN FOR US.
YOU THINK IT IS EASY FINDING AN ENTIRE FLEET OF SHIPS TO TRANSPORT SO MANY GREEKS?
DOES THE ARMY WISH TO REMAIN HERE, XENOPHON?
THE RETURN OF CHEIRISOPHUS MANAGED TO STOP THE BLEEDING, BUT THE DAMAGE WAS ALREADY DONE.
WE SAILED ACROSS THE BLACK SEA AND THEN DISEMBARKED AT HERACLEA TO CONTINUE ON FOOT.

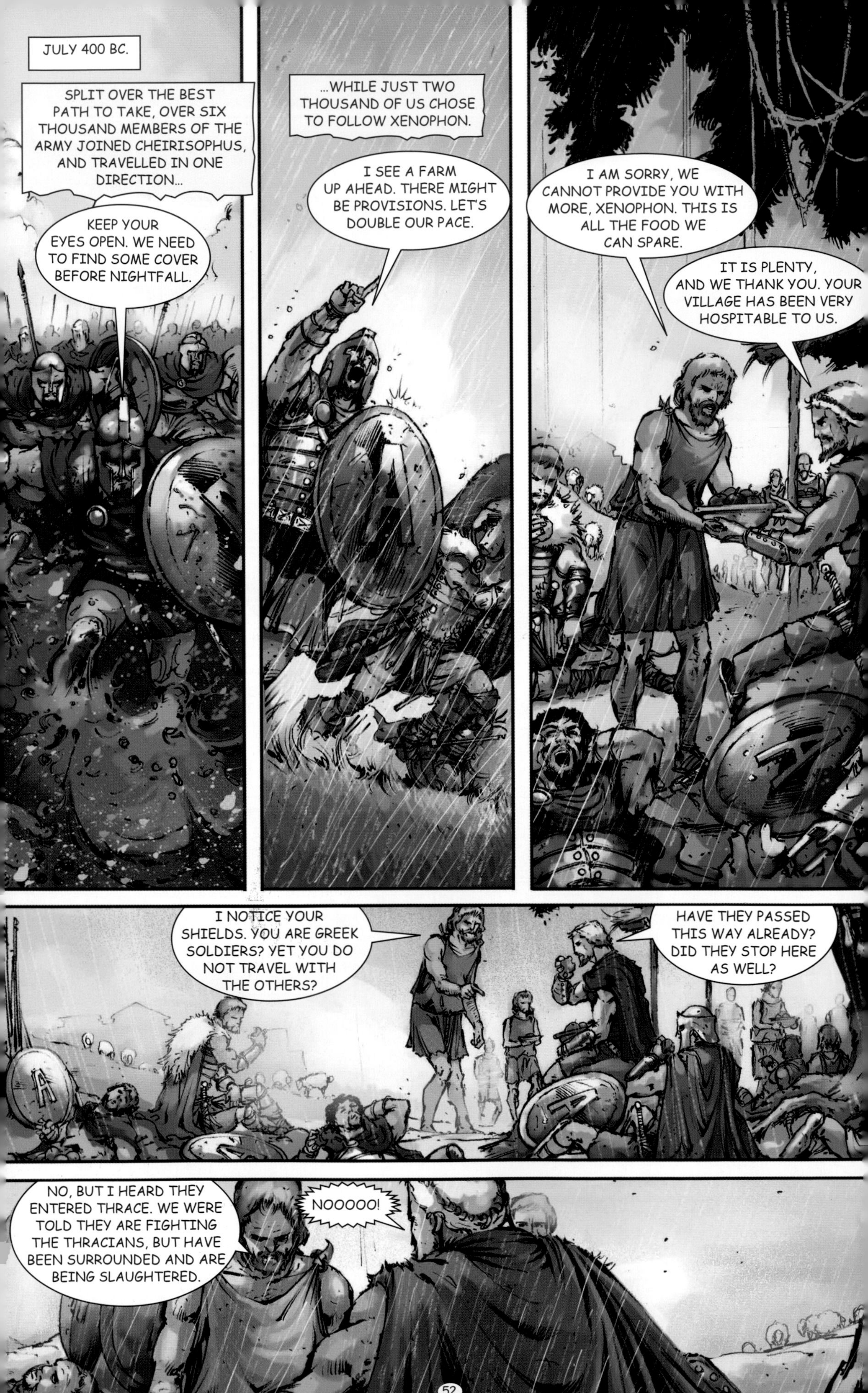
JULY 400 BC.
SPLIT OVER THE BEST PATH TO TAKE, OVER SIX THOUSAND MEMBERS OF THE ARMY JOINED CHEIRISOPHUS, AND TRAVELLED IN ONE DIRECTION...
KEEP YOUR EYES OPEN. WE NEED TO FIND SOME COVER BEFORE NIGHTFALL.
...WHILE JUST TWO THOUSAND OF US CHOSE TO FOLLOW XENOPHON.
I SEE A FARM UP AHEAD. THERE MIGHT BE PROVISIONS. LET'S DOUBLE OUR PACE.
I AM SORRY, WE CANNOT PROVIDE YOU WITH MORE, XENOPHON. THIS IS ALL THE FOOD WE CAN SPARE.
IT IS PLENTY, AND WE THANK YOU. YOUR VILLAGE HAS BEEN VERY HOSPITABLE TO US.
I NOTICE YOUR SHIELDS. YOU ARE GREEK SOLDIERS? YET YOU DO NOT TRAVEL WITH THE OTHERS?
HAVE THEY PASSED THIS WAY ALREADY? DID THEY STOP HERE AS WELL?
NO, BUT I HEARD THEY ENTERED THRACE. WE WERE TOLD THEY ARE FIGHTING THE THRACIANS, BUT HAVE BEEN SURROUNDED AND ARE BEING SLAUGHTERED.
NOOOOO!

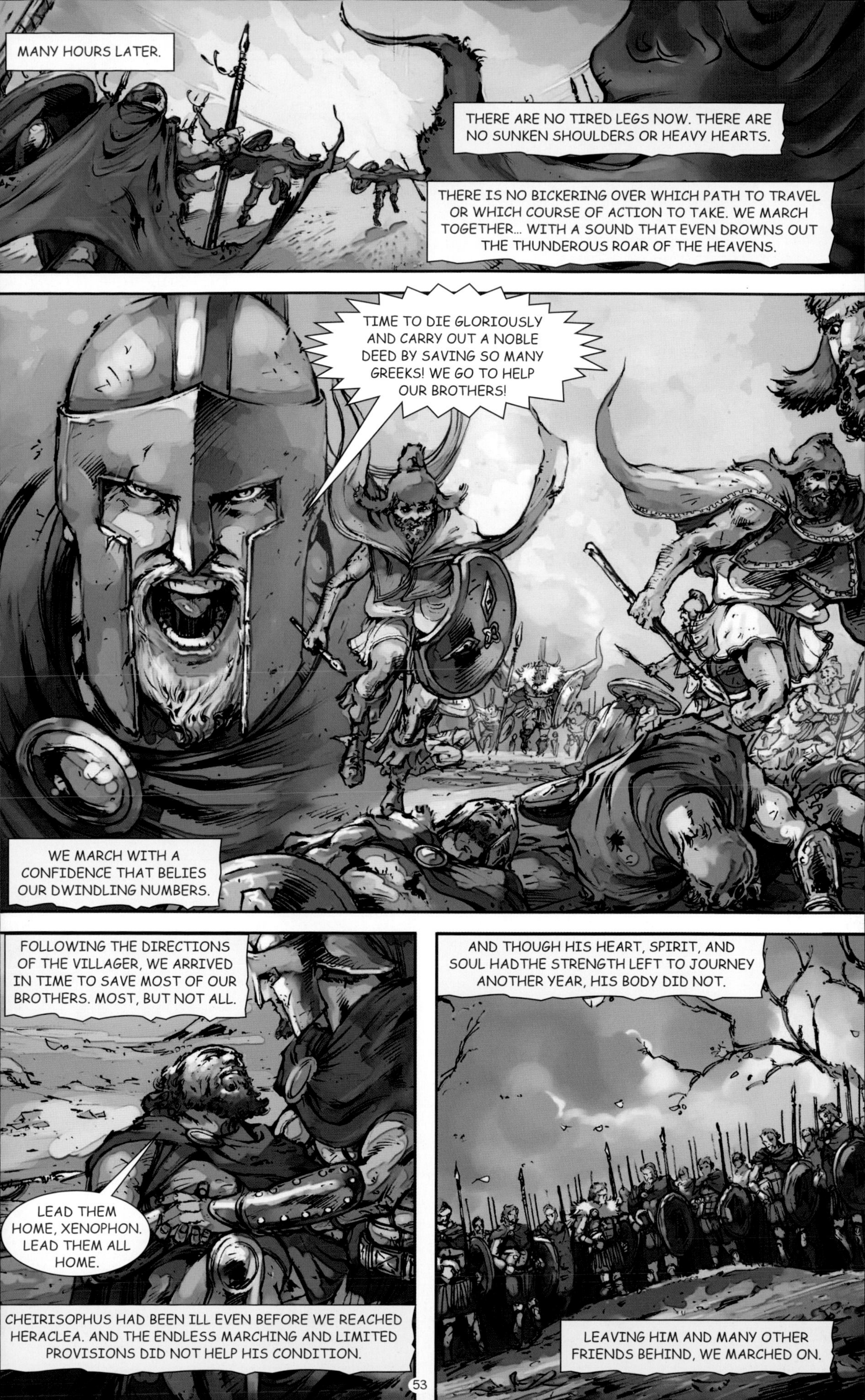
MANY HOURS LATER.
THERE ARE NO TIRED LEGS NOW. THERE ARE NO SUNKEN SHOULDERS OR HEAVY HEARTS.
THERE IS NO BICKERING OVER WHICH PATH TO TRAVEL OR WHICH COURSE OF ACTION TO TAKE. WE MARCH TOGETHER... WITH A SOUND THAT EVEN DROWNS OUT THE THUNDEROUS ROAR OF THE HEAVENS.
TIME TO DIE GLORIOUSLY AND CARRY OUT A NOBLE DEED BY SAVING SO MANY GREEKS! WE GO TO HELP OUR BROTHERS!
WE MARCH WITH A CONFIDENCE THAT BELIES OUR DWINDLING NUMBERS.
FOLLOWING THE DIRECTIONS OF THE VILLAGER, WE ARRIVED IN TIME TO SAVE MOST OF OUR BROTHERS. MOST, BUT NOT ALL.
LEAD THEM HOME, XENOPHON. LEAD THEM ALL HOME.
CHEIRISOPHUS HAD BEEN ILL EVEN BEFORE WE REACHED HERACLEA. AND THE ENDLESS MARCHING AND LIMITED PROVISIONS DID NOT HELP HIS CONDITION.
AND THOUGH HIS HEART, SPIRIT, AND SOUL HADTHE STRENGTH LEFT TO JOURNEY ANOTHER YEAR, HIS BODY DID NOT.
LEAVING HIM AND MANY OTHER FRIENDS BEHIND, WE MARCHED ON.

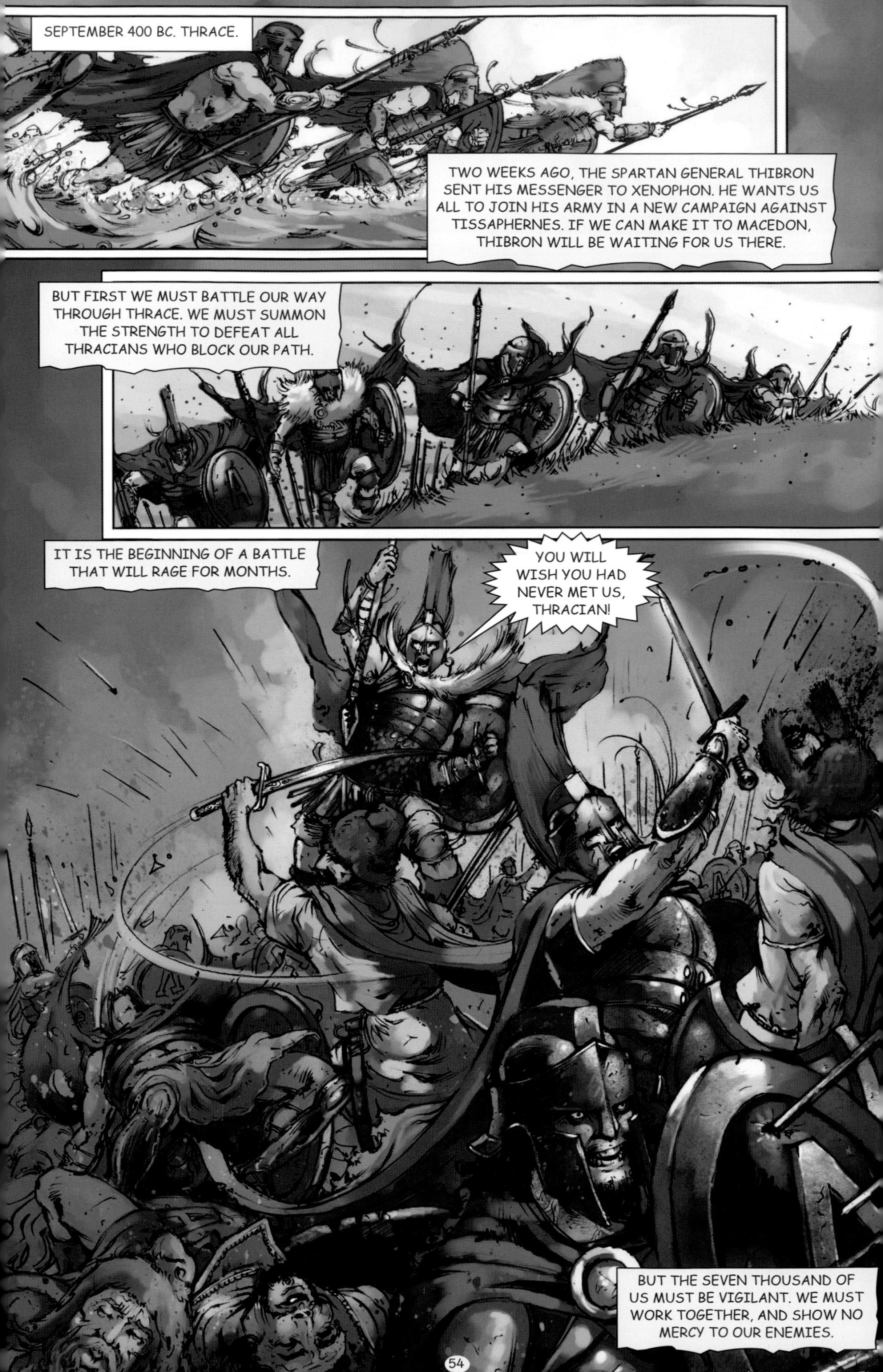
SEPTEMBER 400 BC. THRACE.
TWO WEEKS AGO, THE SPARTAN GENERAL THIBRON SENT HIS MESSENGER TO XENOPHON. HE WANTS US ALL TO JOIN HIS ARMY IN A NEW CAMPAIGN AGAINST TISSAPHERNES. IF WE CAN MAKE IT TO MACEDON, THIBRON WILL BE WAITING FOR US THERE.
BUT FIRST WE MUST BATTLE OUR WAY THROUGH THRACE. WE MUST SUMMON THE STRENGTH TO DEFEAT ALL THRACIANS WHO BLOCK OUR PATH.
IT IS THE BEGINNING OF A BATTLE THAT WILL RAGE FOR MONTHS.
YOU WILL WISH YOU HAD NEVER MET US, THRACIAN!
BUT THE SEVEN THOUSAND OF US MUST BE VIGILANT. WE MUST WORK TOGETHER, AND SHOW NO MERCY TO OUR ENEMIES.

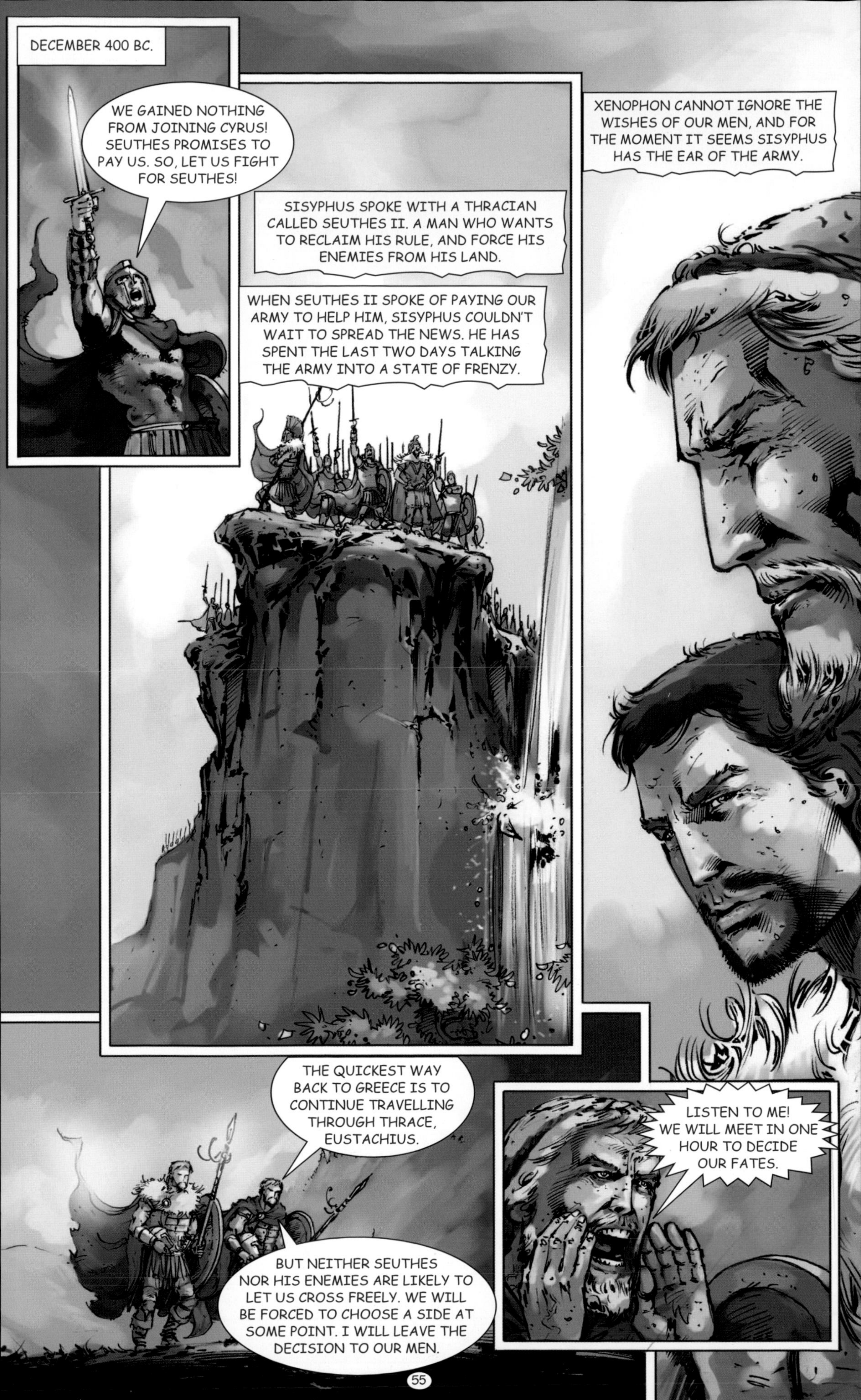
DECEMBER 400 BC.
WE GAINED NOTHING FROM JOINING CYRUS! SEUTHES PROMISES TO PAY US. SO, LET US FIGHT FOR SEUTHES!
SISYPHUS SPOKE WITH A THRACIAN CALLED SEUTHES II. A MAN WHO WANTS TO RECLAIM HIS RULE, AND FORCE HIS ENEMIES FROM HIS LAND.
WHEN SEUTHES II SPOKE OF PAYING OUR ARMY TO HELP HIM, SISYPHUS COULDN'T WAIT TO SPREAD THE NEWS. HE HAS SPENT THE LAST TWO DAYS TALKING THE ARMY INTO A STATE OF FRENZY.
XENOPHON CANNOT IGNORE THE WISHES OF OUR MEN, AND FOR THE MOMENT IT SEEMS SISYPHUS HAS THE EAR OF THE ARMY.
THE QUICKEST WAY BACK TO GREECE IS TO CONTINUE TRAVELLING THROUGH THRACE, EUSTACHIUS.
BUT NEITHER SEUTHES NOR HIS ENEMIES ARE LIKELY TO LET US CROSS FREELY. WE WILL BE FORCED TO CHOOSE A SIDE AT SOME POINT. I WILL LEAVE THE DECISION TO OUR MEN.
LISTEN TO ME! WE WILL MEET IN ONE HOUR TO DECIDE OUR FATES.

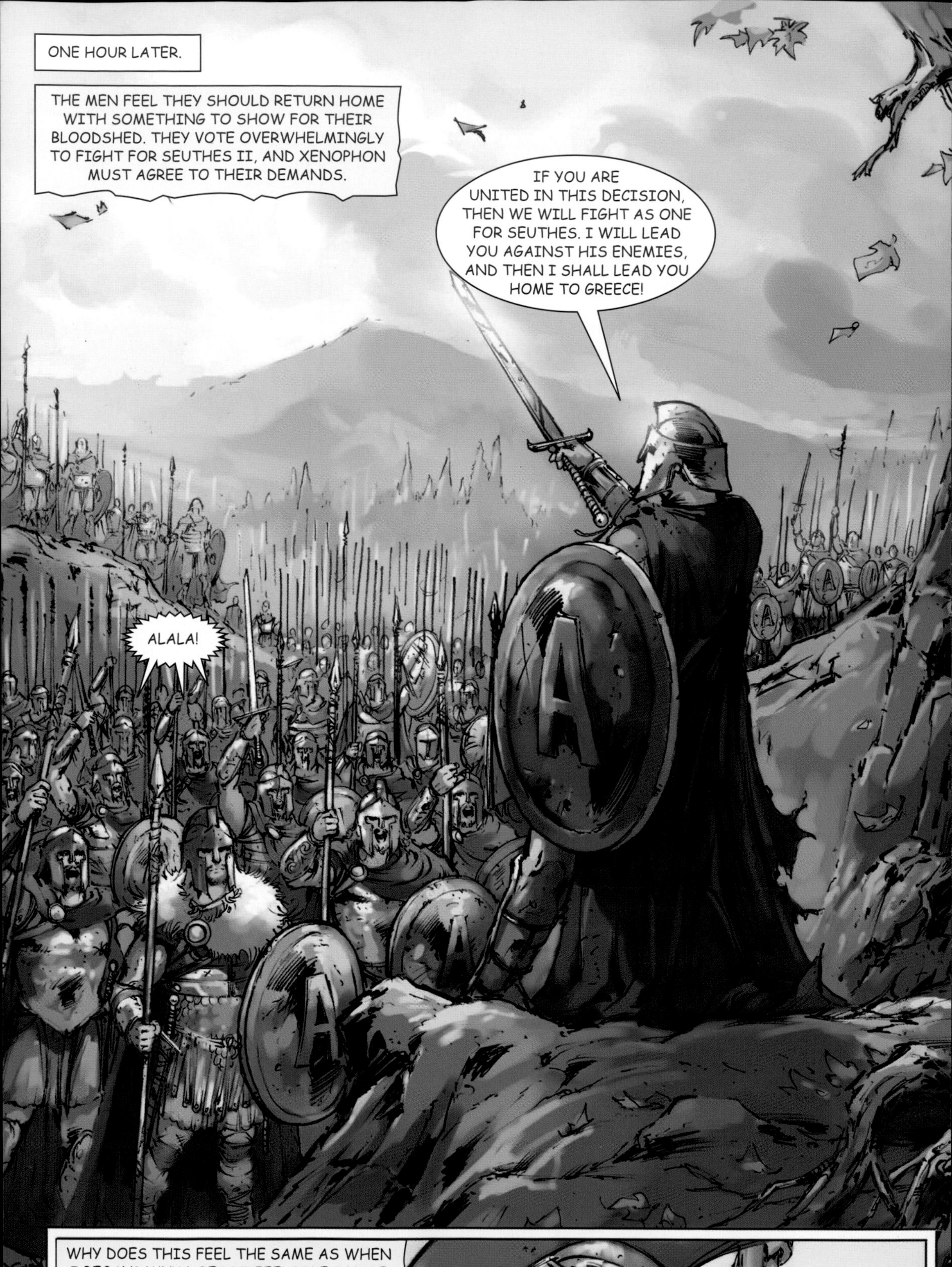
ONE HOUR LATER.
THE MEN FEEL THEY SHOULD RETURN HOME WITH SOMETHING TO SHOW FOR THEIR BLOODSHED. THEY VOTE OVERWHELMINGLY TO FIGHT FOR SEUTHES II, AND XENOPHON MUST AGREE TO THEIR DEMANDS.
IF YOU ARE UNITED IN THIS DECISION, THEN WE WILL FIGHT AS ONE FOR SEUTHES. I WILL LEAD YOU AGAINST HIS ENEMIES, AND THEN I SHALL LEAD YOU HOME TO GREECE!
ALALA!

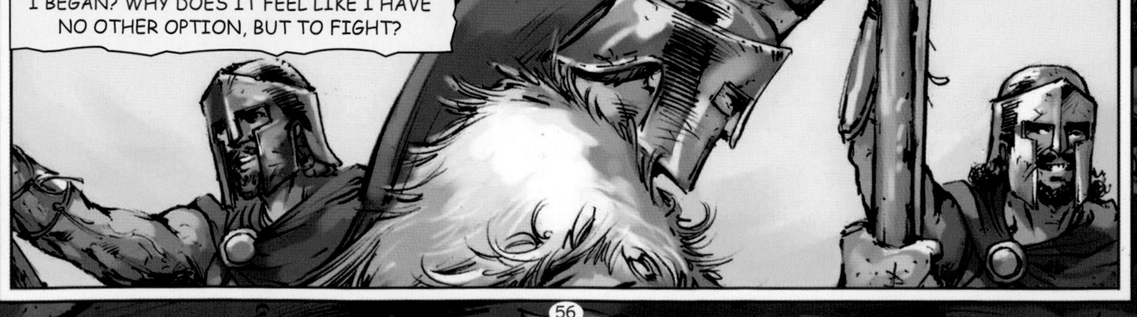
WHY DOES THIS FEEL THE SAME AS WHEN I BEGAN? WHY DOES IT FEEL LIKE I HAVE NO OTHER OPTION, BUT TO FIGHT?

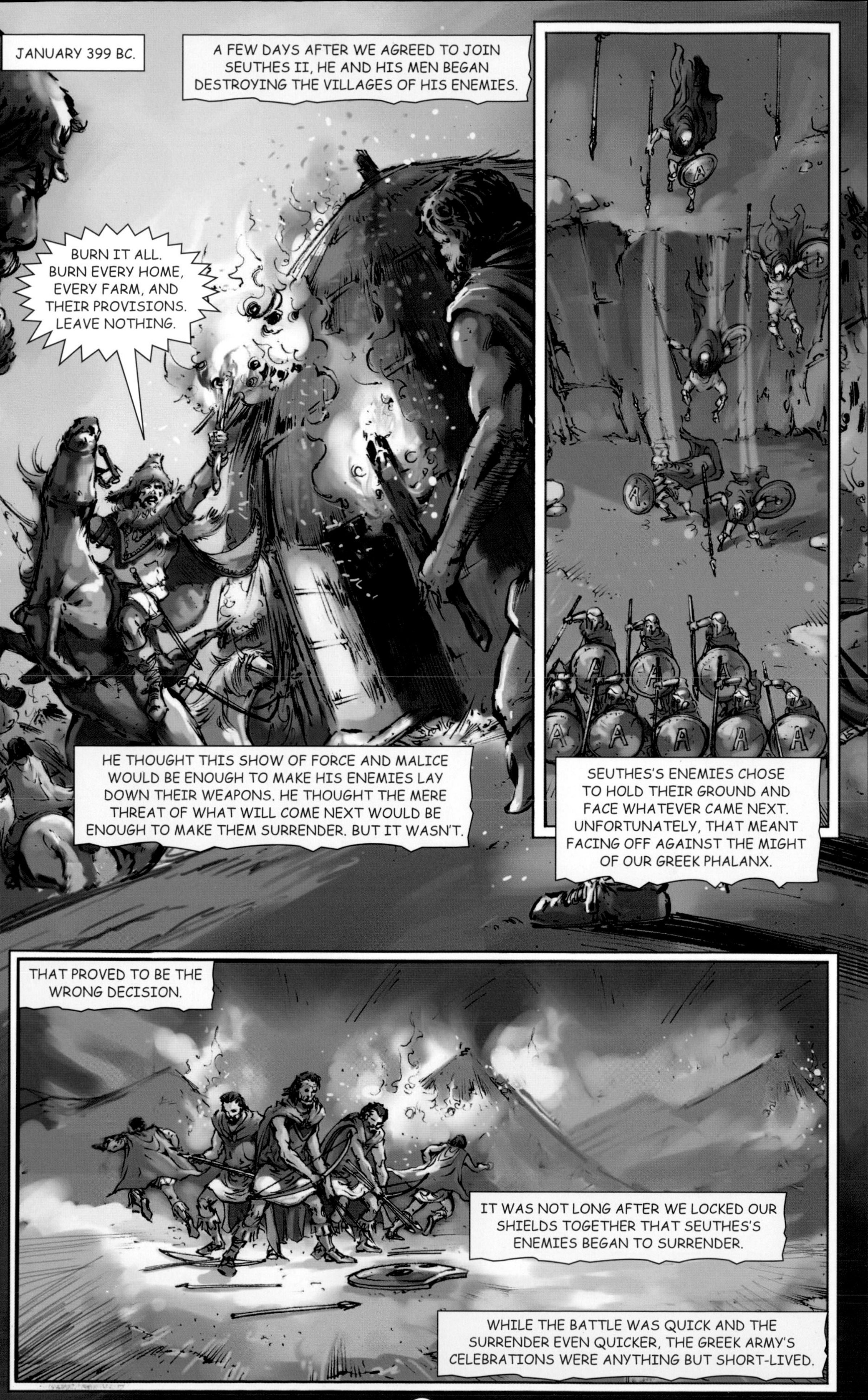
JANUARY 399 BC.
A FEW DAYS AFTER WE AGREED TO JOIN SEUTHES II, HE AND HIS MEN BEGAN DESTROYING THE VILLAGES OF HIS ENEMIES.
BURN IT ALL. BURN EVERY HOME, EVERY FARM, AND THEIR PROVISIONS. LEAVE NOTHING.
HE THOUGHT THIS SHOW OF FORCE AND MALICE WOULD BE ENOUGH TO MAKE HIS ENEMIES LAY DOWN THEIR WEAPONS. HE THOUGHT THE MERE THREAT OF WHAT WILL COME NEXT WOULD BE ENOUGH TO MAKE THEM SURRENDER. BUT IT WASN'T.
SEUTHES'S ENEMIES CHOSE TO HOLD THEIR GROUND AND FACE WHATEVER CAME NEXT. UNFORTUNATELY, THAT MEANT FACING OFF AGAINST THE MIGHT OF OUR GREEK PHALANX.
THAT PROVED TO BE THE WRONG DECISION.
IT WAS NOT LONG AFTER WE LOCKED OUR SHIELDS TOGETHER THAT SEUTHES'S ENEMIES BEGAN TO SURRENDER.
WHILE THE BATTLE WAS QUICK AND THE SURRENDER EVEN QUICKER, THE GREEK ARMY'S CELEBRATIONS WERE ANYTHING BUT SHORT-LIVED.

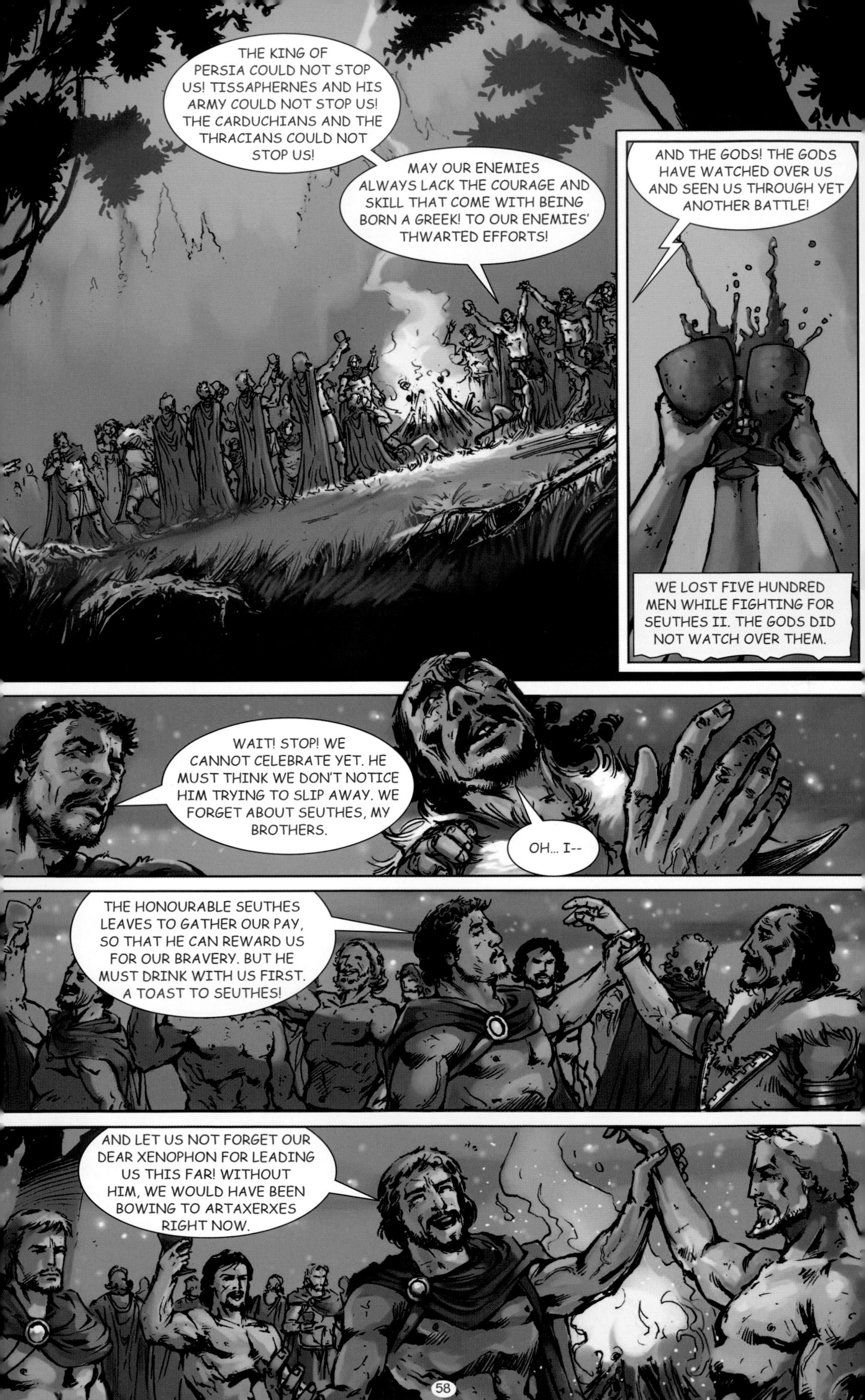
THE KING OF PERSIA COULD NOT STOP US! TISSAPHERNES AND HIS ARMY COULD NOT STOP US! THE CARDUCHIANS AND THE THRACIANS COULD NOT STOP US!
MAY OUR ENEMIES ALWAYS LACK THE COURAGE AND SKILL THAT COME WITH BEING BORN A GREEK! TO OUR ENEMIES' THWARTED EFFORTS!
AND THE GODS! THE GODS HAVE WATCHED OVER US AND SEEN US THROUGH YET ANOTHER BATTLE!
WE LOST FIVE HUNDRED MEN WHILE FIGHTING FOR SEUTHES II. THE GODS DID NOT WATCH OVER THEM.
WAIT! STOP! WE CANNOT CELEBRATE YET. HE MUST THINK WE DON'T NOTICE HIM TRYING TO SLIP AWAY. WE FORGET ABOUT SEUTHES, MY BROTHERS.
OH... I--
THE HONOURABLE SEUTHES LEAVES TO GATHER OUR PAY, SO THAT HE CAN REWARD US FOR OUR BRAVERY. BUT HE MUST DRINK WITH US FIRST. A TOAST TO SEUTHES!
AND LET US NOT FORGET OUR DEAR XENOPHON FOR LEADING US THIS FAR! WITHOUT HIM, WE WOULD HAVE BEEN BOWING TO ARTAXERXES RIGHT NOW.

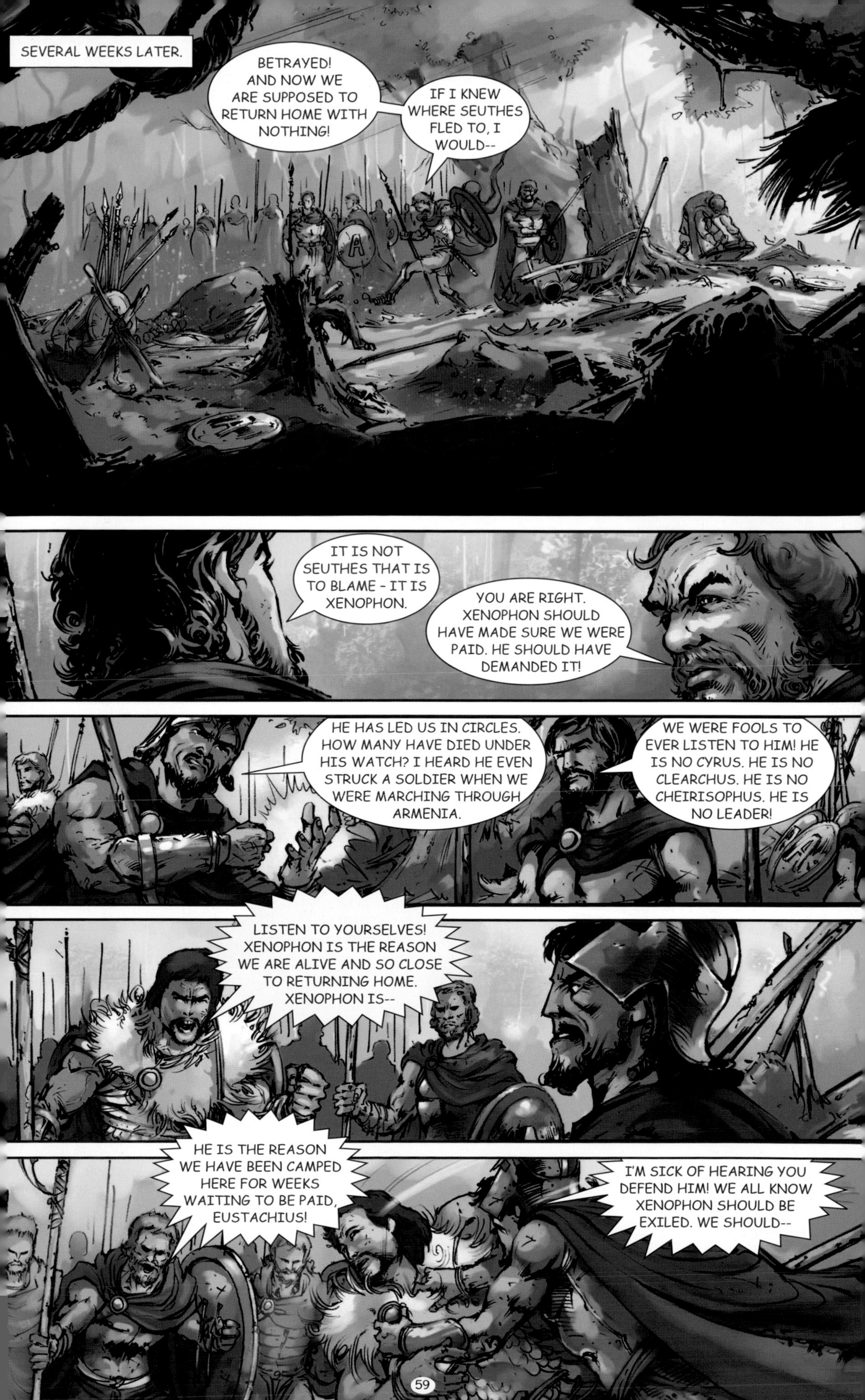
SEVERAL WEEKS LATER.
BETRAYED! AND NOW WE ARE SUPPOSED TO RETURN HOME WITH NOTHING!
IF I KNEW WHERE SEUTHES FLED TO, I WOULD--
IT IS NOT SEUTHES THAT IS TO BLAME - IT IS XENOPHON.
YOU ARE RIGHT. XENOPHON SHOULD HAVE MADE SURE WE WERE PAID. HE SHOULD HAVE DEMANDED IT!
HE HAS LED US IN CIRCLES. HOW MANY HAVE DIED UNDER HIS WATCH? I HEARD HE EVEN STRUCK A SOLDIER WHEN WE WERE MARCHING THROUGH ARMENIA.
WE WERE FOOLS TO EVER LISTEN TO HIM! HE IS NO CYRUS. HE IS NO CLEARCHUS. HE IS NO CHEIRISOPHUS. HE IS NO LEADER!
LISTEN TO YOURSELVES! XENOPHON IS THE REASON WE ARE ALIVE AND SO CLOSE TO RETURNING HOME. XENOPHON IS--
HE IS THE REASON WE HAVE BEEN CAMPED HERE FOR WEEKS WAITING TO BE PAID, EUSTACHIUS!
I'M SICK OF HEARING YOU DEFEND HIM! WE ALL KNOW XENOPHON SHOULD BE EXILED. WE SHOULD--

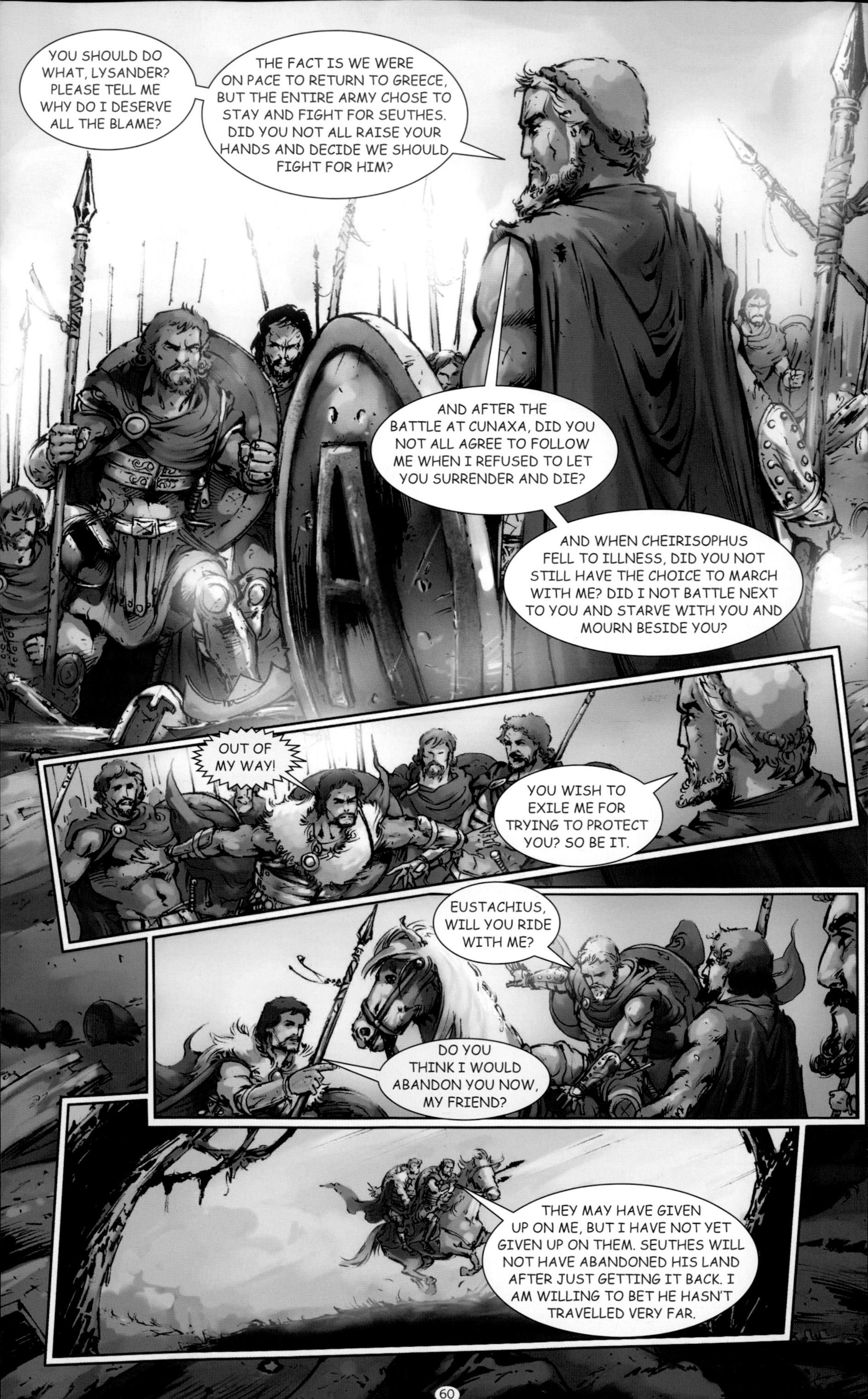
YOU SHOULD DO WHAT, LYSANDER? PLEASE TELL ME WHY DO I DESERVE ALL THE BLAME?
THE FACT IS WE WERE ON PACE TO RETURN TO GREECE, BUT THE ENTIRE ARMY CHOSE TO STAY AND FIGHT FOR SEUTHES. DID YOU NOT ALL RAISE YOUR HANDS AND DECIDE WE SHOULD FIGHT FOR HIM?
AND AFTER THE BATTLE AT CUNAXA, DID YOU NOT ALL AGREE TO FOLLOW ME WHEN I REFUSED TO LET YOU SURRENDER AND DIE?
AND WHEN CHEIRISOPHUS FELL TO ILLNESS, DID YOU NOT STILL HAVE THE CHOICE TO MARCH WITH ME? DID I NOT BATTLE NEXT TO YOU AND STARVE WITH YOU AND MOURN BESIDE YOU?
OUT OF MY WAY!
YOU WISH TO EXILE ME FOR TRYING TO PROTECT YOU? SO BE IT.
EUSTACHIUS, WILL YOU RIDE WITH ME?
DO YOU THINK I WOULD ABANDON YOU NOW, MY FRIEND?
THEY MAY HAVE GIVEN UP ON ME, BUT I HAVE NOT YET GIVEN UP ON THEM. SEUTHES WILL NOT HAVE ABANDONED HIS LAND AFTER JUST GETTING IT BACK. I AM WILLING TO BET HE HASN'T TRAVELLED VERY FAR.

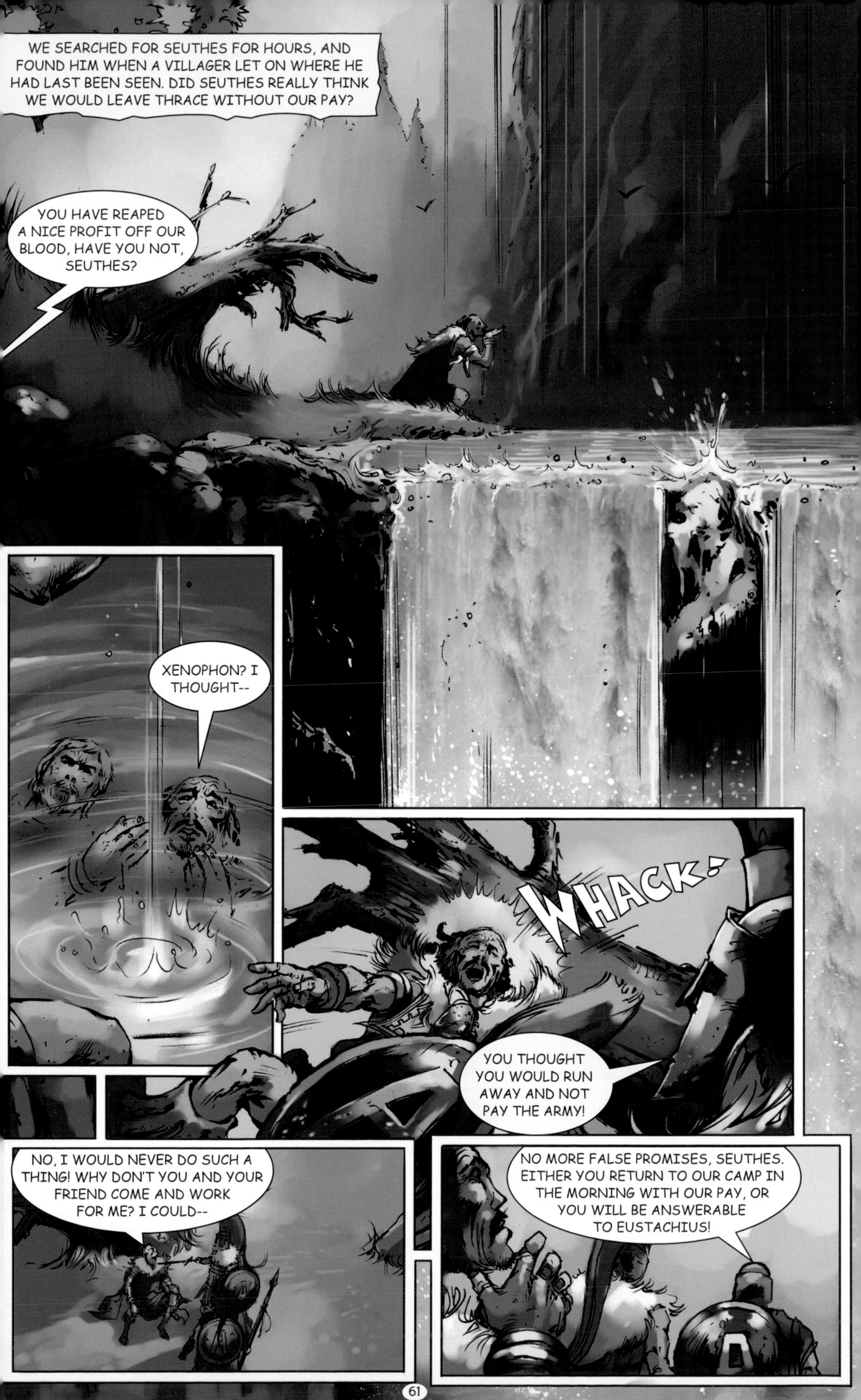
WE SEARCHED FOR SEUTHES FOR HOURS, AND FOUND HIM WHEN A VILLAGER LET ON WHERE HE HAD LAST BEEN SEEN. DID SEUTHES REALLY THINK WE WOULD LEAVE THRACE WITHOUT OUR PAY?
YOU HAVE REAPED A NICE PROFIT OFF OUR BLOOD, HAVE YOU NOT, SEUTHES?
XENOPHON? I THOUGHT--
WHACK!
YOU THOUGHT YOU WOULD RUN AWAY AND NOT PAY THE ARMY!
NO, I WOULD NEVER DO SUCH A THING! WHY DON'T YOU AND YOUR FRIEND COME AND WORK FOR ME? I COULD--
NO MORE FALSE PROMISES, SEUTHES. EITHER YOU RETURN TO OUR CAMP IN THE MORNING WITH OUR PAY, OR YOU WILL BE ANSWERABLE TO EUSTACHIUS!

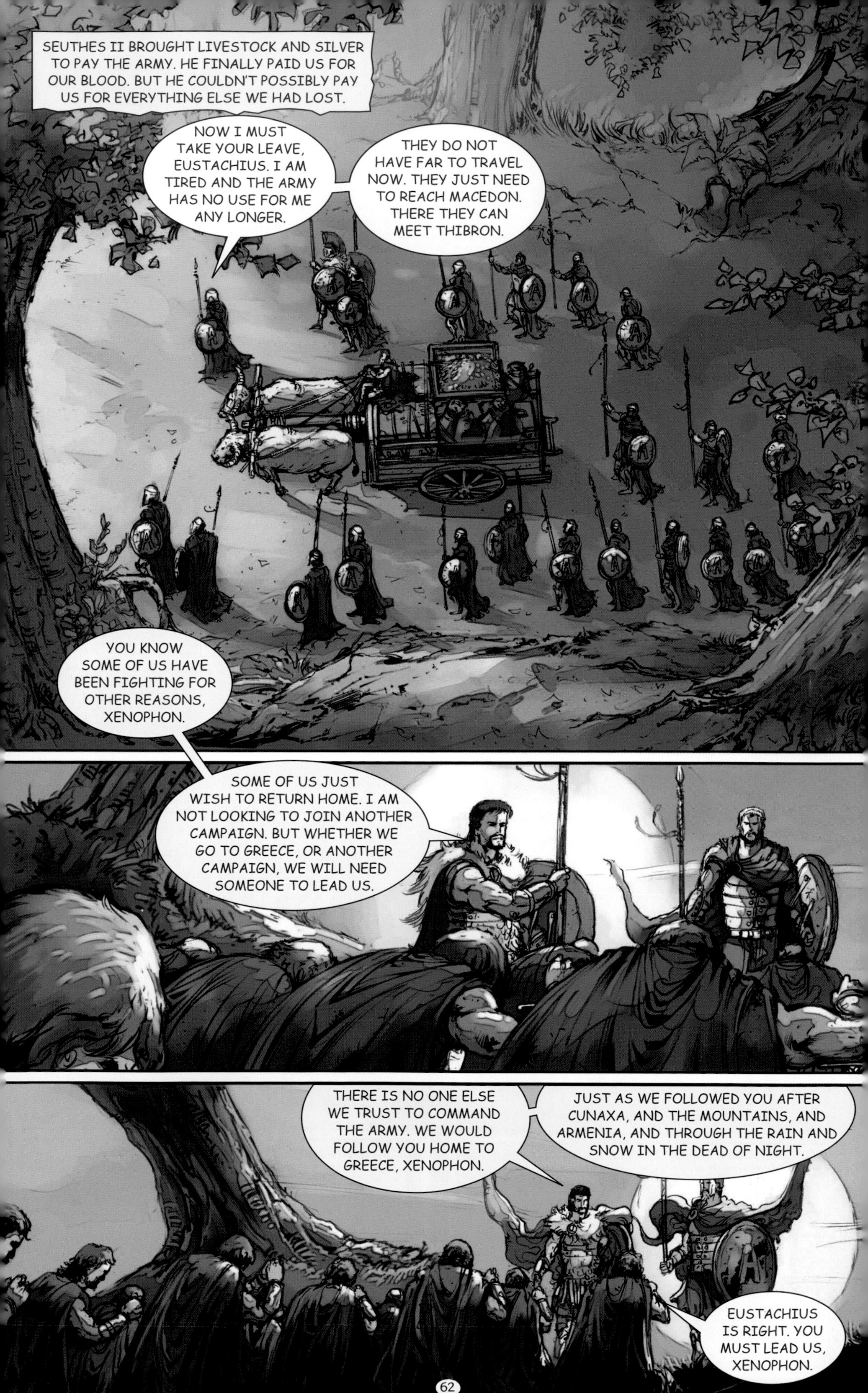
SEUTHES II BROUGHT LIVESTOCK AND SILVER TO PAY THE ARMY. HE FINALLY PAID US FOR OUR BLOOD. BUT HE COULDN'T POSSIBLY PAY US FOR EVERYTHING ELSE WE HAD LOST.
NOW I MUST TAKE YOUR LEAVE, EUSTACHIUS. I AM TIRED AND THE ARMY HAS NO USE FOR ME ANY LONGER.
THEY DO NOT HAVE FAR TO TRAVEL NOW. THEY JUST NEED TO REACH MACEDON. THERE THEY CAN MEET THIBRON.
YOU KNOW SOME OF US HAVE BEEN FIGHTING FOR OTHER REASONS, XENOPHON.
SOME OF US JUST WISH TO RETURN HOME. I AM NOT LOOKING TO JOIN ANOTHER CAMPAIGN. BUT WHETHER WE GO TO GREECE, OR ANOTHER CAMPAIGN, WE WILL NEED SOMEONE TO LEAD US.
THERE IS NO ONE ELSE WE TRUST TO COMMAND THE ARMY. WE WOULD FOLLOW YOU HOME TO GREECE, XENOPHON.
JUST AS WE FOLLOWED YOU AFTER CUNAXA, AND THE MOUNTAINS, AND ARMENIA, AND THROUGH THE RAIN AND SNOW IN THE DEAD OF NIGHT.
EUSTACHIUS IS RIGHT. YOU MUST LEAD US, XENOPHON.

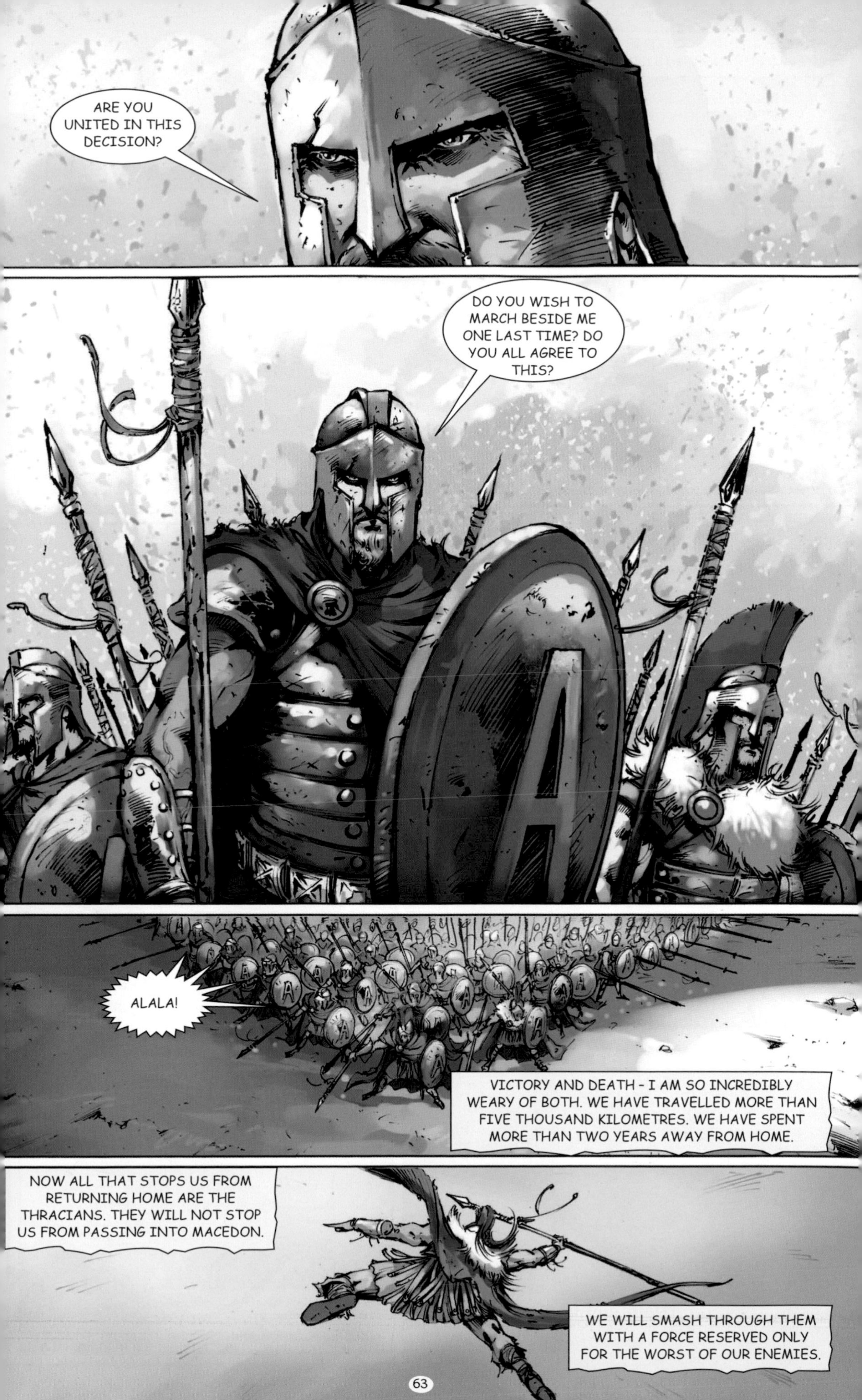

ARE YOU UNITED IN THIS DECISION?
DO YOU WISH TO MARCH BESIDE ME ONE LAST TIME? DO YOU ALL AGREE TO THIS?
ALALA!
VICTORY AND DEATH - I AM SO INCREDIBLY WEARY OF BOTH. WE HAVE TRAVELLED MORE THAN FIVE THOUSAND KILOMETRES. WE HAVE SPENT MORE THAN TWO YEARS AWAY FROM HOME.
NOW ALL THAT STOPS US FROM RETURNING HOME ARE THE THRACIANS. THEY WILL NOT STOP US FROM PASSING INTO MACEDON.
WE WILL SMASH THROUGH THEM WITH A FORCE RESERVED ONLY FOR THE WORST OF OUR ENEMIES.

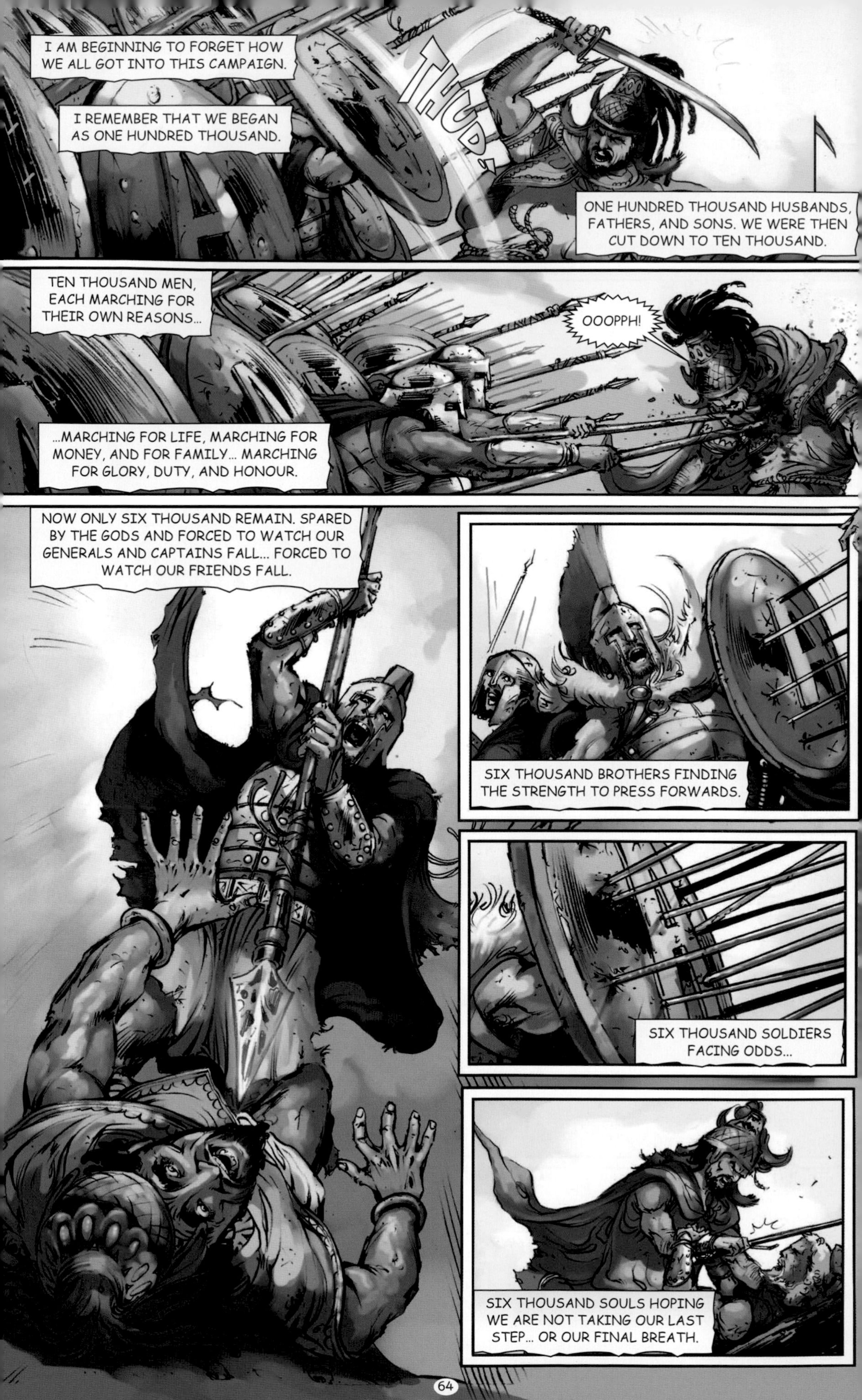
I AM BEGINNING TO FORGET HOW WE ALL GOT INTO THIS CAMPAIGN.
I REMEMBER THAT WE BEGAN AS ONE HUNDRED THOUSAND.
THUD!
ONE HUNDRED THOUSAND HUSBANDS, FATHERS, AND SONS. WE WERE THEN CUT DOWN TO TEN THOUSAND.
TEN THOUSAND MEN, EACH MARCHING FOR THEIR OWN REASONS...
OOOPPH!
...MARCHING FOR LIFE, MARCHING FOR MONEY, AND FOR FAMILY... MARCHING FOR GLORY, DUTY, AND HONOUR.
NOW ONLY SIX THOUSAND REMAIN. SPARED BY THE GODS AND FORCED TO WATCH OUR GENERALS AND CAPTAINS FALL... FORCED TO WATCH OUR FRIENDS FALL.
SIX THOUSAND BROTHERS FINDING THE STRENGTH TO PRESS FORWARDS.
SIX THOUSAND SOLDIERS FACING ODDS...
SIX THOUSAND SOULS HOPING WE ARE NOT TAKING OUR LAST STEP... OR OUR FINAL BREATH.

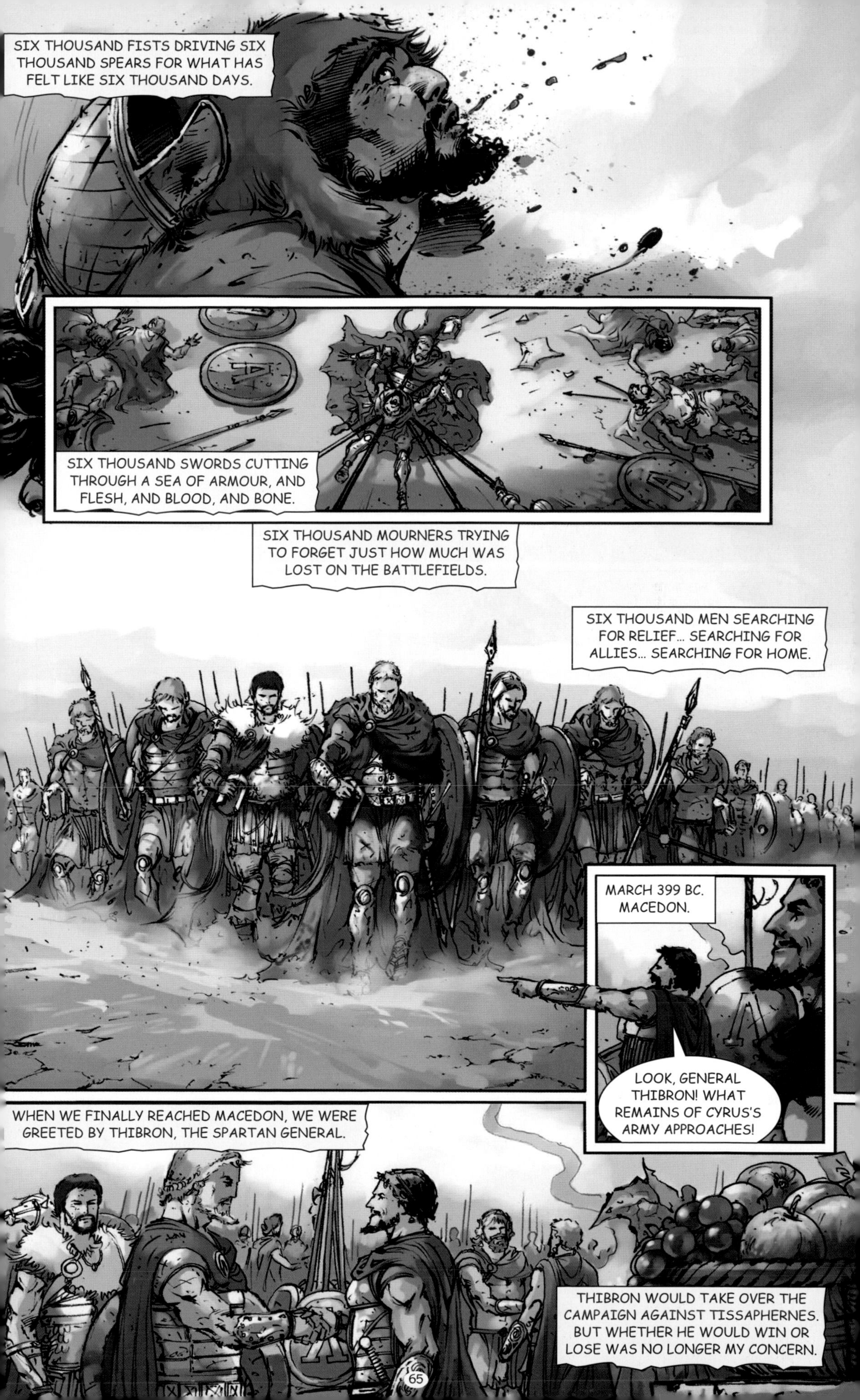
SIX THOUSAND FISTS DRIVING SIX THOUSAND SPEARS FOR WHAT HAS FELT LIKE SIX THOUSAND DAYS.
SIX THOUSAND SWORDS CUTTING THROUGH A SEA OF ARMOUR, AND FLESH, AND BLOOD, AND BONE.
SIX THOUSAND MOURNERS TRYING TO FORGET JUST HOW MUCH WAS LOST ON THE BATTLEFIELDS.
SIX THOUSAND MEN SEARCHING FOR RELIEF... SEARCHING FOR ALLIES... SEARCHING FOR HOME.
MARCH 399 BC. MACEDON.
LOOK, GENERAL THIBRON! WHAT REMAINS OF CYRUS'S ARMY APPROACHES!
WHEN WE FINALLY REACHED MACEDON, WE WERE GREETED BY THIBRON, THE SPARTAN GENERAL.
THIBRON WOULD TAKE OVER THE CAMPAIGN AGAINST TISSAPHERNES. BUT WHETHER HE WOULD WIN OR LOSE WAS NO LONGER MY CONCERN.

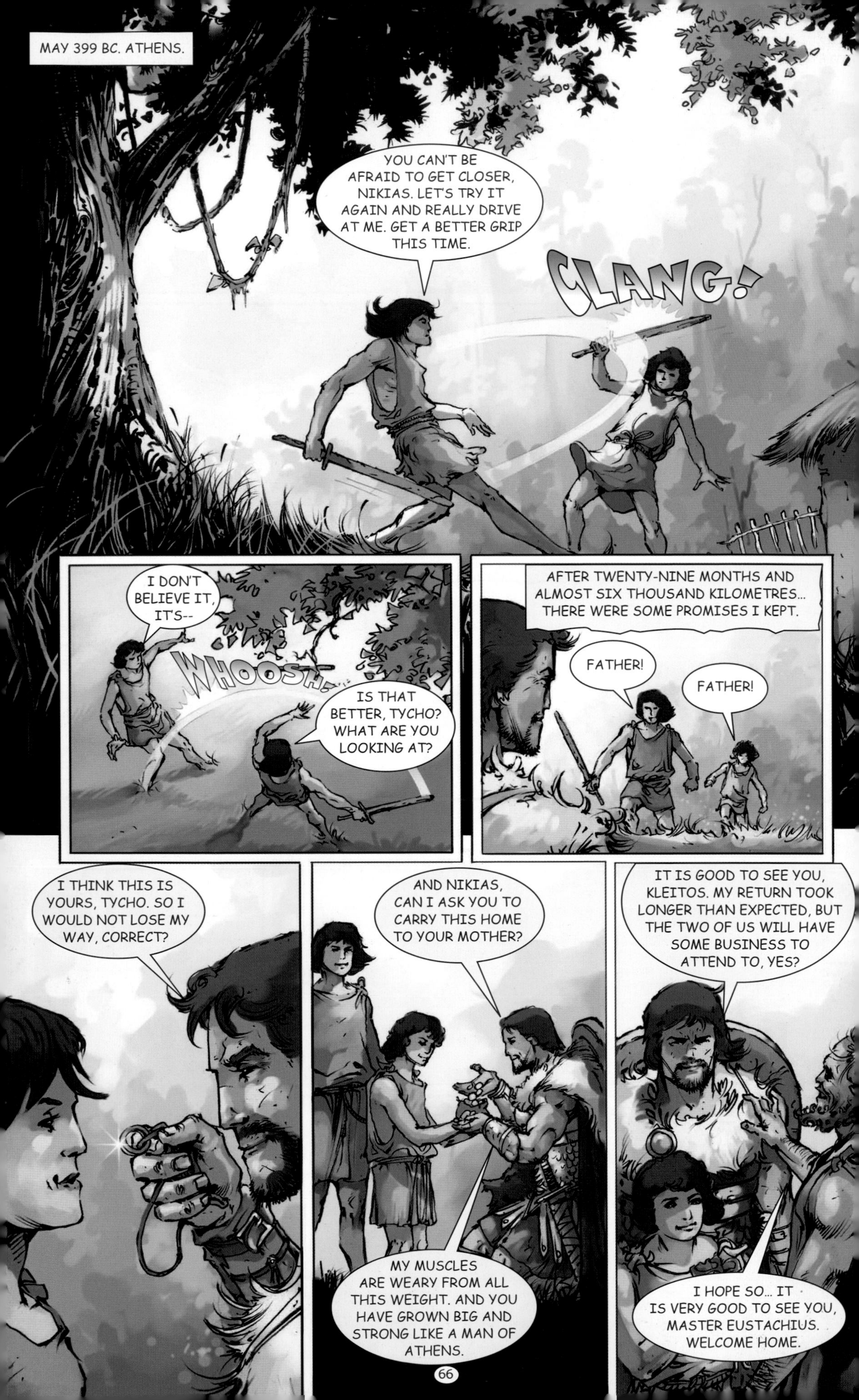
MAY 399 BC. ATHENS.
YOU CAN'T BE AFRAID TO GET CLOSER, NIKIAS. LET'S TRY IT AGAIN AND REALLY DRIVE AT ME. GET A BETTER GRIP THIS TIME.
CLANG!
I DON'T BELIEVE IT, IT'S--
WHOOSH!
IS THAT BETTER, TYCHO? WHAT ARE YOU LOOKING AT?
AFTER TWENTY-NINE MONTHS AND ALMOST SIX THOUSAND KILOMETRES... THERE WERE SOME PROMISES I KEPT.
FATHER!
FATHER!
I THINK THIS IS YOURS, TYCHO. SO I WOULD NOT LOSE MY WAY, CORRECT?
AND NIKIAS, CAN I ASK YOU TO CARRY THIS HOME TO YOUR MOTHER?
MY MUSCLES ARE WEARY FROM ALL THIS WEIGHT. AND YOU HAVE GROWN BIG AND STRONG LIKE A MAN OF ATHENS.
IT IS GOOD TO SEE YOU, KLEITOS. MY RETURN TOOK LONGER THAN EXPECTED, BUT THE TWO OF US WILL HAVE SOME BUSINESS TO ATTEND TO, YES?
I HOPE SO... IT IS VERY GOOD TO SEE YOU, MASTER EUSTACHIUS. WELCOME HOME.

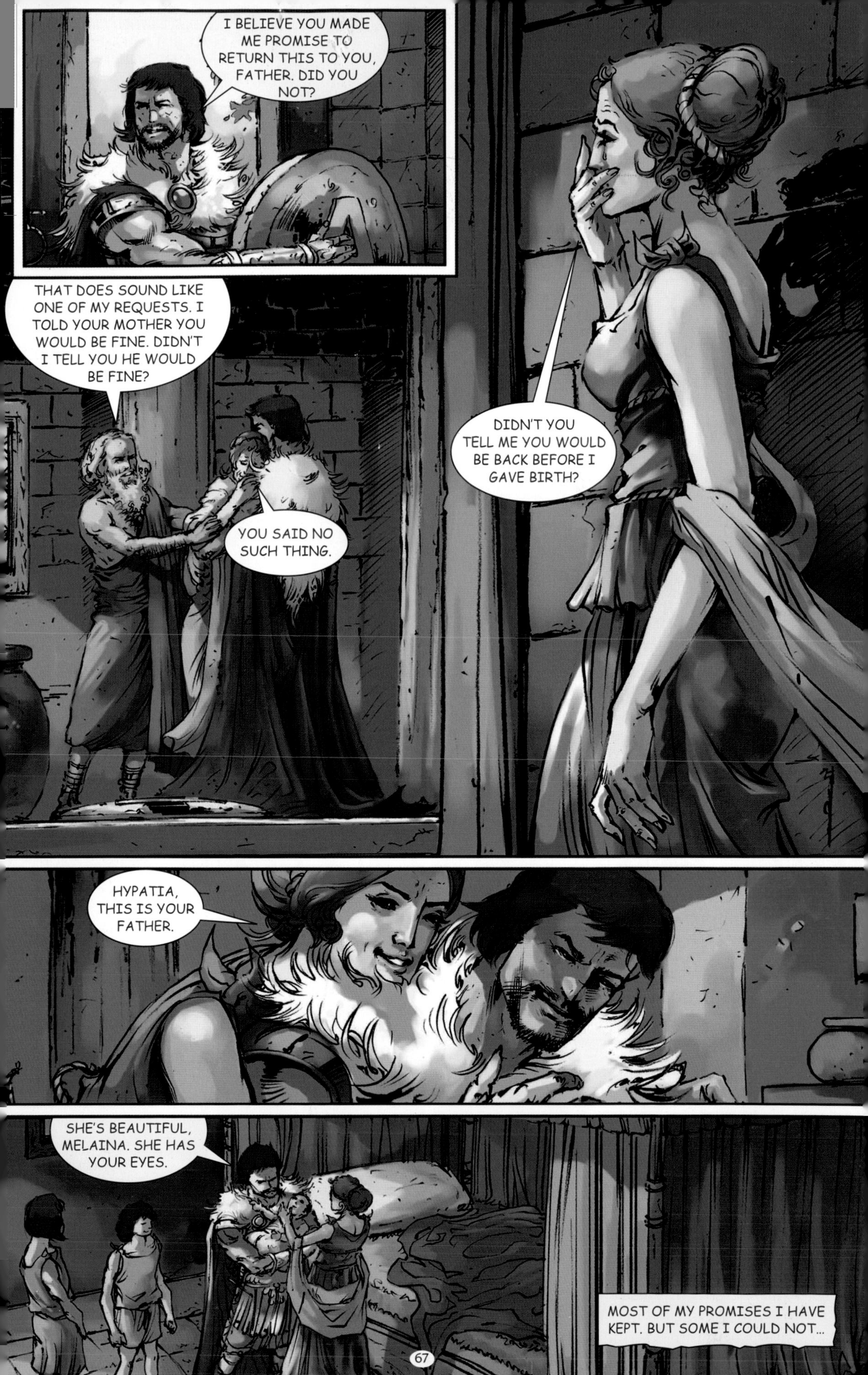
I BELIEVE YOU MADE ME PROMISE TO RETURN THIS TO YOU, FATHER. DID YOU NOT?
THAT DOES SOUND LIKE ONE OF MY REQUESTS. I TOLD YOUR MOTHER YOU WOULD BE FINE. DIDN'T I TELL YOU HE WOULD BE FINE?
YOU SAID NO SUCH THING.
DIDN'T YOU TELL ME YOU WOULD BE BACK BEFORE I GAVE BIRTH?
HYPATIA, THIS IS YOUR FATHER.
SHE'S BEAUTIFUL, MELAINA. SHE HAS YOUR EYES.
MOST OF MY PROMISES I HAVE KEPT. BUT SOME I COULD NOT...

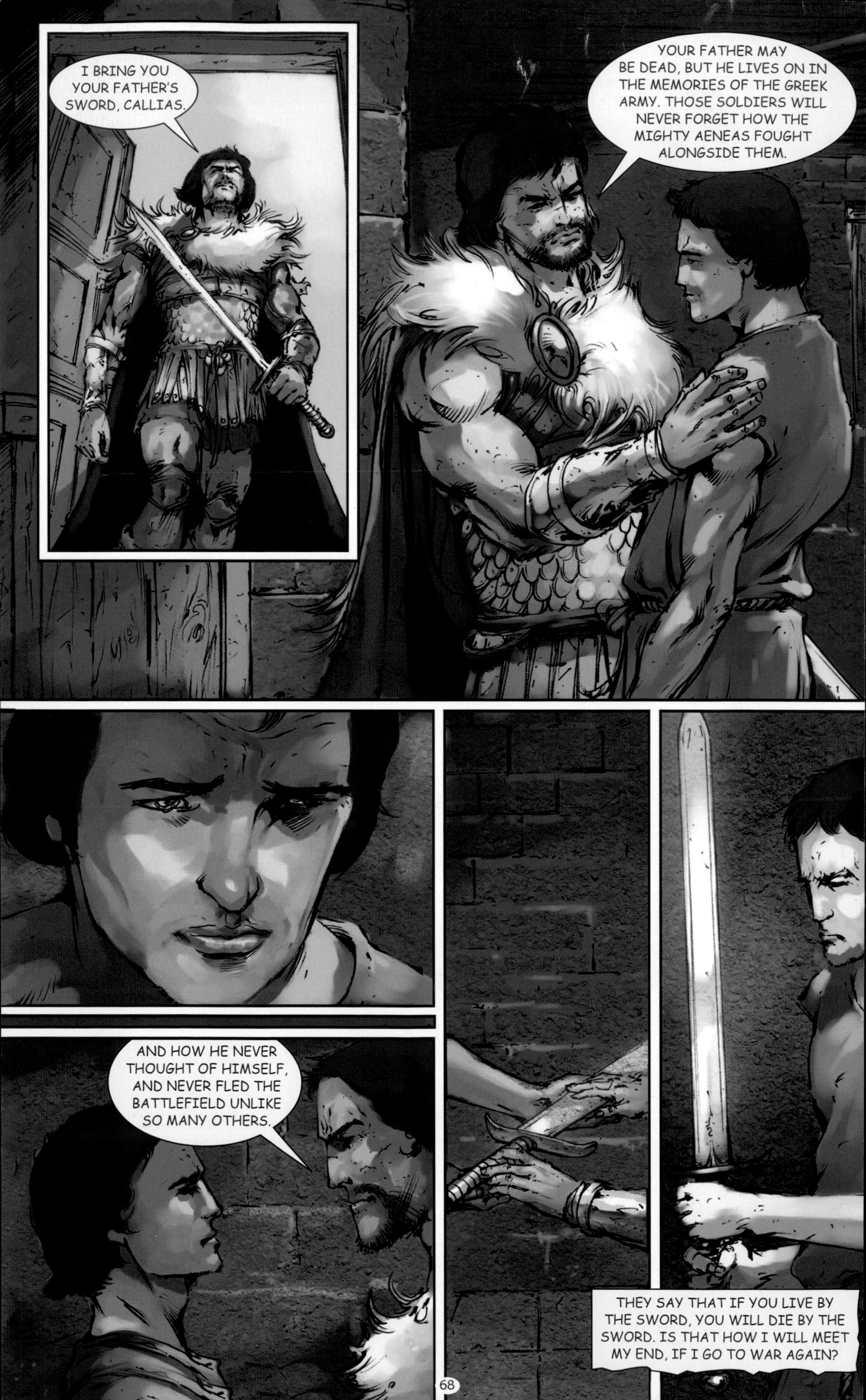
I BRING YOU YOUR FATHER'S SWORD, CALLIAS.
YOUR FATHER MAY BE DEAD, BUT HE LIVES ON IN THE MEMORIES OF THE GREEK ARMY. THOSE SOLDIERS WILL NEVER FORGET HOW THE MIGHTY AENEAS FOUGHT ALONGSIDE THEM.
AND HOW HE NEVER THOUGHT OF HIMSELF, AND NEVER FLED THE BATTLEFIELD UNLIKE SO MANY OTHERS.
THEY SAY THAT IF YOU LIVE BY THE SWORD, YOU WILL DIE BY THE SWORD. IS THAT HOW I WILL MEET MY END, IF I GO TO WAR AGAIN?

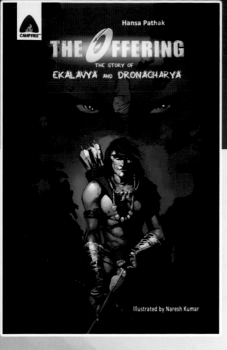

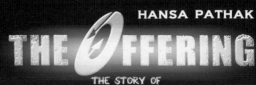

Hansa Pathak
THE OFFERING
THE STORY OF
EKALAVYA AND DRONACHARYA
Illustrated by Naresh Kumar

HANSA PATHAK

THE OFFERING

THE STORY OF EKALAVYA AND DRONACHARYA

ILLUSTRATED BY NARESH KUMAR

An exemplary story from the *Mahabharata* that conveys the power of determination and self-discipline.

The *Mahabharata* is an abiding collection of stories about the ancient Pandava-Kaurava feud over the Kuru throne. Traditionally, the Pandavas are accepted as the good side but there is one story that drops an ungraceful shadow on that notion – and that is the story of Ekalavya. Ekalavya, whose skill with archery could have rescued the Kauravas from defeat. Ekalavya, who gave away his most important asset as *guru dakshina* so that the *guru-shishya parampara* is not let down.

The story of Ekalavya features in the *Mahabharata* years before the battle of Kurukshetra, when the Pandavas were still learning warfare under Dronacharya. The story begins simply – the tribal prince seeks the tutelage of Guru Dronacharya, only to incite the jealously of Arjun – but ends terribly.

Narad, the great *rishi*, who despises lies but loves trouble, is determined to make this story of Ekalavya live on. And it is on the battlefield of Kurukshetra, where the rectification of injustice was sought at all costs, that he chooses to retell the tale.

CAMPFIRE™

www.campfire.co.in

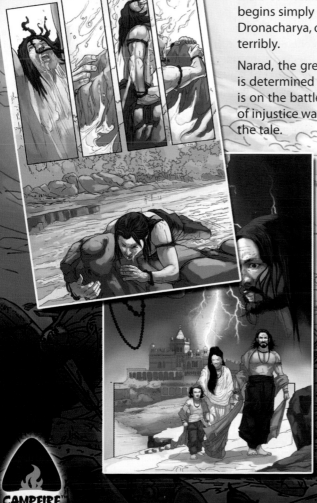

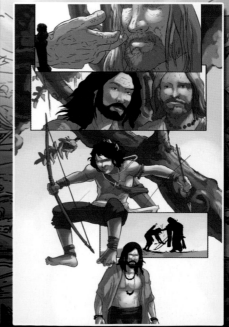

ANCIENT WARRIORS

SPARTANS

One Spartan was worth several men of any other state – that is how strong the Spartans in the 6th to 4th centuries BC were considered to be. One of the most disciplined, well-trained, and feared military forces, the Spartans were expected to return only victorious or dead from a war. If not, they were considered cowards and were punished with death or banishment.

Just before they went to war, the wives or mothers of Spartan warriors presented them a shield which said, 'With this, or upon this.' This was a very important custom for them and it meant that they were either supposed to return victorious with the shield or their dead bodies were to be brought back on the shield. The Spartan boys were drilled from infancy in military training. The Spartan male had to pass a difficult test of fitness, military ability, and leadership skills to become a full citizen and a Spartan soldier. The training lasted for twelve years, and their service did not end till they reached the age of sixty. Spartan soldiers, who died in combat during a victorious campaign, were granted headstones.

ATHENIANS

Arts, music, and intellectual pursuits were common among the citizens of Athens. But alongside their education in arts and science, Athenian boys were given military training too. An Athenian soldier's rank was decided by his social or economic status. Athenian soldiers only trained for two years and were required to serve only two years in the military – one in the garrison and one in a border fort. But men over twenty years of age could be called up for military service whenever required. The Athenian army was no match for the size and effectiveness of the Spartan army, but what they lacked on land, they made up for at sea. They were experts at naval warfare and soon rose to become the dominant naval power for a century or more.

PERSIANS

The Persian army was made up of Persians, Medians, and Assyrians. The archers and cavalry troops were the backbone of the Persian army. The unique feature of this army was the vast number of people that comprised it. Not only the juniors, but commanders, dignitaries, and Persian nobility also participated in actual fighting.

The training of a member of the Persian nobility consisted of running, swimming, horse grooming, tilling the land, tending the cattle, making various handicrafts, and getting accustomed to standing at watch. He would be trained in the arts of the chase (both on foot and on horseback), archery, throwing the spear and javelin, and of sustaining forced marches in unfriendly climate. The military profession of a young Persian started at twenty and continued till the age of fifty as a foot soldier or a rider.

DESIGN YOUR OWN SHIELD

A shield is one of the most important parts of a soldier's armoury. Alongside being strong and protective, the shield should look brilliant and represent the soldier's strength and valour.

Given on your left is a knight's shield. It may offer protection from a fire-spewing dragon but it looks so blank and boring. Copy the design on a piece of paper and use your imagination to make the shield look interesting and meaningful. You can draw bold designs on the border, fill your choice of colours in the space between the first and second circles, and draw symbols (like a lion, a scorpion, the sun, etc.) that mean something important to you at the centre of the shield.

XENOPHON

Though the story and most of the characters of *400 BC* are fictional, Cyrus the Younger, Artaxerxes II, and Xenophon were real people.

Xenophon was a Greek historian and philosopher. He was born into a wealthy Athenian family in 430 BC. He was highly influenced by Socrates in his early life. At the age of twenty-two, he became a military commander and led a group of mercenary soldiers (those who fight for whoever would pay them) to Persia. They fought for Cyrus, the younger brother of King Artaxerxes of Persia, against the Persian army. After Cyrus was killed, they were driven out of Persia. Xenophon was the force behind the Athenian army and led them through many dangerous adventures back to their homeland. Xenophon occupied a conspicuous position in society. As he was both energetic and enterprising and led many expeditions, his personal history and exploits attracted great attention even while he lived. Later in life, he wrote various historical memoirs such as the *Anabasis* and the *Cyropædia*.